TOILING UNDER THE SUN

ALSO BY COREY EMORY

Concerning The Dust

TOILING UNDER THE SUN

A NOVELLA

COREY EMORY

PORTOBELLO ROAD PUBLISHING

This is a work of fiction. Unless otherwise indicated, all of the names, characters, dialogue, businesses, places, events, and incidents in this book are either the product of the author's imagination or used in a fictitious manner. They are not intended to refer to any living persons or to disparage any person's, company's, school's, or institution's products or services. No portions of this book were generated using Artificial Intelligence (AI).

ISBN 13: 9798218816230

Library of Congress Control Number: 2025921116

Portobello Road Publishing, Cambria, CA

Awareness is the enemy of sanity, for once you hear the screaming, it never stops.

— Emilie Autumn

Romantic agony in literature may be compared with the manic-depressive syndrome in psychology, with ecstasy as its counterpart. It flourishes where conventional religion is dead, as in the worlds of Sade, Lautréamont, Huysmans, Rimbaud, Baudelaire, where the possibility of comparable sensation to the "religious experience" must be sought elsewhere.

— Richard Seaver, Terry Southern, and Alexander Trocchi, eds.
Writers In Revolt: An Anthology

There is a particular kind of pain, elation, loneliness, and terror involved in this kind of madness. When you're high it's tremendous. The ideas and feelings are fast and frequent like shooting stars, and you follow them until you find better and brighter ones. Shyness goes, the right words and gestures are suddenly there, the power to captivate others a felt certainty. There are interests found in uninteresting people. Sensuality is pervasive and the desire to seduce and be seduced irresistible. Feelings of ease, intensity, power, well-being, financial omnipotence, and euphoria pervade one's marrow—

But, somewhere, this changes. The fast ideas are far too fast, and there are far too many; overwhelming confusion replaces clarity. Memory goes. Humor and absorption on friends' faces are replaced by fear and concern. Everything previously moving with the grain is now against—you are irritable, angry, frightened, uncontrollable, and enmeshed totally in the blackest caves of the mind. You never knew those caves were there. It will never end, for madness carves its own reality.

— Kay Redfield Jamison, *An Unquiet Mind: A Memoir of Moods and Madness*

OVERTURE

I'm drowning. Can you see me? Something is wrong, my mind ... will I be lost forever? Keep counting ... that is the arrangement, the pattern that is easily followed; it is the way to move through. The. Escalating. Deterioration. Of. Reason. The intellectual dizziness. Keep counting. No focus, no clarity until the counting starts. That's the way through, the way to clarity, into the open night ... don't you want to breathe?

"Sami ... Sami ... they are going to hurt you ... can't you hear that ... you are ... you're collapsing, Sami ... listen to the sounds ... you're collapsing." One, two, three—

"Sami." I think someone is calling my name. Four, five, six—

"Sami." Seven, eight, nine—

"Why are you screaming?" Ten, eleven, twelve—

"Stop screaming." Thirteen, fourteen—

"Oh, look Sami, the bright green leaves of young oaks are blowing in the summer breeze. Just there, not far now, look, the path splits; it pours out in two directions. The path. Comes apart. Oak trees. Fire."

A summer breeze, there are a number of ways through, but the math needs to be correct, keep counting, see that man standing in the forest, look, there is a rabbit caught, was caught, is caught, now catching, now caught, can't you understand, there is a rabbit caught by the throat in a barbed confrontation. No, wait, it's caught by the paw, it's your paw, why are you crying little rabbit, the breeze is gushing through the leaves, loud, like rushing water ... watch the outline of the leaves against the flames of the large oak. The mountains are steep, dark, covered by large redwoods hundreds of years old. Summer comes from the East. The trees are quiet. There is a large lake. Look at the swimming pool surrounded by ancient redwoods and quiet maples; the water is clear and never needs cleaning except for the leaves and sometimes a drowned squirrel. Who is that lying face down in the pool?

It's a young girl, Sami ... how did you drown, Sami ... look how pretty your auburn hair is, it's swirling so gently around your pale face, her pale face, my pale face, your pale face, keep counting. What is that story in your hand, Sami ... did you read it ... *The Chrysanthemums*, Sami? Look, there is a young boy sitting on a lounge chair ... he is singing quietly. He is reading ... didn't you give him the short story ... the sun is setting; he is watching the burning leaves drift down into the pool. He is smiling; that old oak tree is burning. Keep counting, Sami; ashes from the tree are cascading around him, and the pages of the story are fluttering in the summer wind. Look, he is getting up; he is stretching.

"Sami."

He is looking at the girl in the pool.

"Sami." I think he is whispering to you. He is looking at your hair. Look how nice your dress is, and your face is so clean, so pale. He is looking at the burning oak tree, fifteen, sixteen, seventeen, keep counting, always count, it's the way home, the numbers have to be correct. Smell the woods ... smell the summer wind, it's stirring all the leaves, it's sweeping across the pool; the smell of the woods mixing with the clean scent of chlorine ... breathe in slowly, Sami. The woods, the pool, eighteen, nineteen, who is the girl, her hair is illuminated by the fire. Look Sami, they are melting together ... do you remember summer ... keep counting, you are not real ...

"Sami, would you describe your thoughts as unusual?" an older man sitting across from me asks. I look at him briefly. Twenty, twenty-one, twenty-two, his hair is brown and carefully brushed to one side. He is wearing an expensive-looking suit. He is staring at me from across a desk. He is looking at me encouragingly, and I want to tell him I'm thirsty and need water, but I can't seem to bring the appropriate energy to mind. I only visualize water, visualize my thirst ... all the emotion ... all the meaning in the idea seems gone. I don't care that I'm thirsty. Thirsty ... I'm not sure I know what you mean ... don't you want to ask for water? Something in my mind is dissolving; there is danger somewhere behind me, sounds ... like whispering ... deep revulsion is crashing through me.

"Sami," the man says. I stare at him. "Do you remember the question?"

"I'm not sure ... " I hear myself say. The words are sluggish; they stumble in my mouth. I try to keep my voice steady, but there is a slight break, a tiny fracture in the last word. Twenty-three, twenty-four. I can feel the man watching me carefully.

"Sami ... do you understand you tried to harm yourself?" he asks. But I'm only dimly aware that he is asking me a question. My mind does not register the content of the question.

"Well ... why don't you tell me some of the things you see?" he says. There's a pause. Why are you afraid to ask for water ... why did you wear a dress today? You are weak in a dress.

"Sami ... " the man's voice again ... he is looking at me, "It's okay to talk freely." There is another pause, another momentary silence, and I'm trying to remember something ...

"Can you tell what you see, Sami?" the man asks. Start over, one, two, three, four, five, six, seven—

"I see my brother," eight, nine, ten, eleven ...

"What about your brother?" he asks. His voice seems far away, and I feel the room slowly tighten—there— something slipping into the room ... in the sunlight ... coming in through the window. I'm being watched.

"It seems so hazy," I hear myself say. First, looking at the man, then, looking out the window momentarily, and finally, turning back to the man sitting across from me.

"Sami, your mother is out in the hallway. I'm going to bring her in with us. Is that okay with you?" the man asks. I nod. He leaves the room, and a moment later, they both walk in. My mother comes over to me and gives me a hug and kisses my cheek. Twelve, thirteen, fourteen. She's been crying. The man is talking to her, asking her questions, and I'm trying to pay attention to what they are saying, but there is an impression, in my mind, of a small point of light. I close my eyes and try to focus on the light. It's slowly growing bigger and bigger. The light is radiant and feels impossibly bright. I can hear the man and my mother talking, but somehow, they don't seem important anymore. And as the light gets brighter, I can feel a warm flutter begin to spread out from the center of my heart.

"Have you noticed any behavior from Sami," the man is asking my mother, "that might indicate a disassociation from reality ... any habits ... um, patterns ... or certain ways of doing things? ... For example, does she feel like she needs to face a certain direction when sleeping, or perhaps she feels compelled to perform certain, um, rituals ... hand signals ... or something like that ... so that nothing bad will happen to her ... maybe she believes she will be lost?" he asks, and my mother is answering, and the light is getting brighter and brighter, and the warm flutter in my heart is getting more intense—

A sound cuts across my mind ... voices. Mumbling. The light is gone. The warmth is gone. And I sense, more than see, a darkness rushing in, replacing the light and the warmth. I open my eyes and try to remember the last number. Fourteen, no fifteen ... no fourteen.

"Does she believe she can predict things?" the man is asking. "Does she believe something is controlling her—her thoughts?" Fifteen, sixteen, seventeen. The questions continue, but I'm unable to zero in, to focus. "Does she have trouble distinguishing between reality and fantasy? Does she hear things? Does she smell things? Does she see things? Does she believe she has special abilities? Does she think people can read her mind? Does she think she's in danger? How long have there been signals?" he asks.

"Symptoms of increasing decline over the last two years," my mother says, and I wonder where my father is. I wonder why he's not here.

"Would you describe Sami as having strong emotional states, perhaps moments of euphoria? Does she notice ... things ... see people ... that no one else can see? Does she have conversations with people who aren't there? I would like to try some long-term medication," he says. Keep counting, Sami—eighteen, nineteen, twenty ...

CHAPTER 1

I was thirteen when I first became curious about paintings. It was late August, 1953 at my grandparent's house in Palm Springs, and a heatwave with daily temperatures of over a hundred degrees and unusually high humidity had been going, nonstop, for almost two weeks.

Most days, my mother, father, and grandparents, on my father's side, would sit under the large patio umbrella in the backyard and sip Tom Collins; my mother would just drink gin. My little brother, who was six, would try to catch lizards with long grass, a trick my grandfather taught us, but mostly, he would be in the swimming pool.

One afternoon, I walked out back and saw my grandfather sitting alone under the large umbrella, and he was holding a small painting. His eyes were closed, and his chin was resting against his chest. He opened his eyes and looked at me when I sat down next to him. I'd seen the painting hanging in his study.

"*Courtyard with Lunatics* ... Francisco Goya," he said sipping the Tom Collins. "It's just a copy ... Goya wasn't commissioned to paint it. He painted it on his own." He looked first at me, then the swimming pool, then finally up at the San Jacinto Mountains.

"That's important to understand ... very important," he said, mumbling the last two words. He handed me the painting, "Try to imagine the sounds in that moment." I looked at the painting, and I remember feeling uncomfortable, sad, though I didn't understand why.

This memory is what I'm thinking about as I sit across from Dr. Kreeft, an art professor at Fordham who I'm interviewing for a documentary about the relationship between theology, philosophy, and the arts. He is explaining, "The young ... at this time ... are pushing back against the, uh, religious ... and to a lesser extent, against the hard scientific determinism that is so prevalent today." There is a slight pause as the professor thinks for a minute. "They seem to be forsaking the gloomy ... the, uh, pessimistic and domineering constraints of these two opposite belief systems." He pauses again, looks up at nothing. Thinking.

Then, something clicks for him, and he looks back at me. "It may seem very abstract. Dry. Even painfully impractical, but I think it is important to understand that ideas produce actions. Think about the last time you got upset about something ... what were you thinking about, what idea were you upset about? How did you behave as a result? Keeping that in mind, what ideas are the youth ... of this particular generation ... reacting against? Moreover, how do their ideas impact the kinds of art they like and produce? And does this art merely express their ideas and feelings, or does it also create or perhaps reinforce certain, uh, behavior? A new norm? A new Truth ... capital 'T.' Think of art as looking at someone's personal journal," the professor pauses.

He seems to be trying to mentally summarize his points and looks down at a piece of paper in front of him. "As the development of art and its subjects, especially as it pertains to and attempts to struggle with the development of philosophy in the

Western ... uh ... ethos," he says hesitatingly, clearly searching for the right word, the right idea.

I watch him quietly, not interrupting, not coaching or trying to steer the conversation. I want his responses to be natural and genuine. I wonder if he and my grandfather would have gotten along—what Dr. Kreeft would say about Francisco's *Courtyard with Lunatics*. I feel nervous; I'm having doubts about the documentary. Doubts about whether or not the artforms, the actual way in which artists express themselves, can really answer the questions asked in art ... I'm worried that beauty cannot speak to the longing that never really seems to leave my mind.

"This generation is choosing the hope of romantic idealism ... look, think of it this way, on one side you have the moral, the ethical, the western philosophical language and ideas, including the ideas of organized religion ... and on the other side, you have the meaninglessness that results from scientific determinism, to say nothing of the impact of the first and second World Wars. Now, you have a whole generation of young people looking at these two options and saying, 'No ... we choose spiritualism, we choose a love that cannot be held by religious—normative—language. We choose Romeo and Juliet,'" he pauses here and looks first at me then into the camera just above my left shoulder. "It's as if they are saying, 'organized religion, western philosophy, and scientific determinism are comparable to the House of Montague and the House of Capulet. With religion and western philosophy representing the House of Montague and scientific determinism representing the House of Capulet ... but the young people are rejecting both both houses, rejecting the strictness of both families and choosing to follow after Romeo and Juliet." He pauses again. "Or perhaps it's more accurate to say that they choose the poets likes Jack Kerouac ... Arthur Rimbaud ... it's not a perfect analogy." He smiles holding his hands up like as if saying, "What can you do?"

"I've been teaching in the art department, here at Fordham, for over twenty years. This is the first time I have seen and sensed an utter rejection of organized religion and scientific thought," he finishes.

"Can you give me an example of what you are describing?" I ask, attempting to gently steer him back to the topic, the theme, the primary reason for the documentary—art as a means of spiritual experience.

"Yes. Consider American painters from the 40s and 50s ... there was a strong momentum toward what is called expressionism. This movement actually started in the late 1800s, predominantly in Paris ... for example, Renoir ... Monet, but the thing to keep in mind is that this movement is simultaneously a philosophical idea and a style of painting. Think of Byzantine art from about 330-730 A.D. Christians, believing in a Christian God, painted pictures that depicted their beliefs ... see? Christianity is both an idea and a style of painting. So, what are the expressionists saying? Put simply, expressionists are rejecting 'normative' forms of painting, but really, it is a rejection of philosophical, theological, and scientific rules, uh, laws ... norms, if you will." He pauses. "There are two things happening at once. First, there is the rejection of old-world norms, and second, there is a push, a need, for meaning ... in a meaningless world ... expressionism boils down the art—at least it is trying to do so—to a blurry picture in hopes that a 'principle' will be the only thing that stands out, and this principle will give meaning."

He pauses again and seems to realize something and quickly adds, "of course, this is only my opinion. There are endless interpretations of what modern art means and what it may or may not be trying to communicate ... uh ... I guess I'm only trying to show, for the sake of this documentary, how philosophy influences art ... I'm thinking of artists like Adolph Gottlieb, Robert Motherwell, Mark Rothko, Jackson Pollock ... they are searching for meaning ... to see 'behind the veil' as it were."

I make a note to "show examples of these painters ... possibly overlaid during fade-out with a voice-over observation from one of the professors I have already interviewed."

"The kids today are in the same boat as these painters," he continues. "They are rejecting old-world norms while searching for meaning ... they are saying, 'sex is real, drugs are real, alcohol is real, music is real ... and these together make up a new, true, and genuine spiritual experience, and this new spiritual experience gives a sense of meaning and therefore a sense of hope.'"

I look down at my notes then at my assistant, Mary. She nods; we have the information we need, and the actual filming is good. She whispers in the cameraman's ear, and he stops filming.

I look back at Dr. Kreeft and smile. "Thank you for your time, Dr. Kreeft. I know you are busy, and we really appreciate you taking the time to talk with us. You've helped greatly in explaining the influence of philosophy on art," I say standing up. I am disappointed that he never really described how art ... beauty can be a means of spiritual experience ... what William James described as "mystical experience." I was hoping for a way past the normal experiences of art, beyond what I might feel if I walked into the Cathedral of Saint Mary of the Flower in Florence—something more than just theology or historical stories expressed in paintings and architecture. I'm annoyed that he didn't really say if direct interactions with God through beauty are even realistic ... the Catholic mystics say that they are possible but are ineffable.

He comes around the desk and shakes my hand. "I'm curious. Who else have you interviewed?"

"Three philosophy professors from three different universities, two professors of theology, and two art professors ... you are my last interview," I say. He smiles but seems disappointed that I didn't name the professors or the universities.

"What's next for you ... when will the documentary come out?"

"We will need to film some paintings ... examples from the artists you have mentioned in this interview," I say but don't bother mentioning that post-production will take a couple months and then the documentary will be released. We shake hands again as the crew finishes packing up.

CHAPTER 2

L ater that afternoon, I am sitting in my hotel room, drinking gin and tonic, my third, and smoking a cigarette ... both habits I picked up from my mother. A message for me at the front desk said that a woman named Barbara, in L.A., would like to talk with me about a possible project and to "please return my call at your earliest convenience." I look at the piece of paper with Barbara's message and phone number and wonder how she knew where to contact me. I turn back to photographs of paintings that we have included in the documentary. An hour later I'm on the phone with Barbara. She says she works for Thomas Lane, and Thomas is interested in hiring me for a political documentary.

"I'm not a political filmmaker," I say. "I have no experience in that area."

"We know," she says. "We know you specialize in ecological and aesthetic subjects." There is a slight pause. "That's why Thomas is interested in hiring you ... he appreciates the ... grassroots ... feel of your documentaries," she says and informs me that Thomas has "significant financial backing" from "third parties." After we hang up, I pour myself another drink and wonder if I should accept the job. I have an urge to call my father and ask him what he thinks. I try to visualize what the job would feel like, look like. I imagine interviewing people on political subjects. Four drinks later, I decide to take the job.

It's one in the morning, and I can't sleep. I'm thinking about the interview with Dr. Kreeft and Romeo and Juliet, and there is a pulse, just there, just behind me; a beat ... a kind of frequency that I can't ignore. I'm having a difficult time discounting a kind of awareness ... truth is dread ... I try to escape this awareness ... the implications. I think of my father. I think of my little brother ... he ... I try to empty my mind, but the thoughts evade my efforts to ignore them. I try to picture my family, try to focus on something that is tangible, real, flesh and blood. I try to picture my father, then my brother, then my mother. Something, I'm not sure what, lifts from my mind, and I can see there is a kind of display, a visual melody ... a living metaphor that is symbolic of this life. Active, violent, confusing ... a perplexity that burns all that is good in my mind to the ground. A barren waste land. The concepts, the sounds, the feelings, the philosophical ideation ... they are always fluctuating, first real, unmovable, then melting, then liquid, then vapor, then nothing.

I remember my mother telling me about a party she went to at Hearst Castle when she was fifteen. It was 1932. She was the youngest person there. It was a cowboy and Indian theme with the women dressed as Indians and the men dressed as cowboys. My mother tells me she was "naïve about the sexual subtlety of the theme—of Indian women being raped by cowboys." Her father, dressed as a cowboy, wouldn't let her dress up as an Indian. She protested but ended up wearing a black shortsleeve dress and black high heels. She walked around the castle trying to ignore the loud laughter of men and women, drunk and half groping each other throughout the castle. She headed down to the Neptune pool. The pool was large, the water pale blue. She stood at the edge and stared into the water. Distant sounds of music and laughter. Surrounding the pool were pillars—a Roman décor.

"Hi," a woman says to my mother.

"Hi."

"What's your name?" the woman asks casually.

"Elizabeth."

"Who are you with?"

"My father."

"What does he do?"

"He's the editor of the *San Francisco Chronicle*."

"I like your dress ... it goes really well with your auburn hair and blue eyes ... you're very pretty ... do you work?"

"I'm in high school; I don't have a job."

"No, I mean do you model?"

"No," she blushes.

"I think you should ... you are very pretty ... your hair color is intoxicating. I'm going to give you my card. It has my personal number on it. Talk to your dad, and see if he would be open to you modeling. I would like to represent you."

I read my mother's life as a kind of advertisement.

CHAPTER 3

Three days later, I'm back in Los Angeles and driving east on the Sunset Strip. The Santa Ana Winds are pushing forcefully down the San Gabriel and San Bernardino Mountains and washing out through the L.A. Valley to the Pacific. My car is actually rocked by the force of the winds, and as I drive on Sunset, an abrupt dread hits me, almost reverberates through me like a loud sound ... a shockwave. I have to pull over and get out of the car. I light a cigarette, my hands trembling slightly from the increasing sense of foreboding and adrenaline. I watch the tall palm trees bend. I take a Nembutal and smoke two more cigarettes before I am able to calm down enough to get back in the car and drive on.

Twenty minutes later, I'm sitting in a waiting room in Studio City, only slightly high on Nembutal. Apprehension still lingers but only vaguely, dimly, in the back of my mind. I look around the waiting room. On one of the walls is a large black-and-white photo of a building. Underneath the photo, on a placard is written, "McComb, Mississippi - City Hall." Next to it is a framed picture of a pretty young black girl in a white dress. Underneath the picture is the name Brenda Travis. Next to her is a picture of a teenage boy. Underneath his picture is the name Emmett Till. Brenda's name sounds vaguely familiar, but I'm not sure why. I have never heard of Emmett Till. On another wall are various photos of young people protesting the Vietnam War. Above these photos, someone has written in large letters, "'We are not to simply bandage the wounds of victims beneath the wheels of injustice, we are to drive a spoke into the wheel itself.' - Dietrich Bonhoeffer." Behind the secretary are three documentary film posters for *The Exiles*, *The Rejected,* and *Nine from Little Rock*. I have seen *The Exiles*. There is also a replica painting of the *Dance of Youth* by Pablo Picasso. Underneath the painting is a quote by the artist: "The purpose of art is washing the dust of daily life off our souls."

The waiting room windows rattle every time there is a strong gust of wind. I stand up and walk over to them. The city spreads out five stories below. I watch a small dust storm moving through the dry streets. The dust storm looks like smoke, and I suddenly remember riding the large Ferris wheel on the Santa Monica Pier when I was twelve years old. It was late December, and the night sky was clear, and the Santa Ana winds were moving offshore at 60 miles an hour. The Ferris wheel's bright neon lights were dazzling … vivid purple and blue, and the Ferris wheel creaked in the wind. As it slowly reached the top of its circuit, I looked out at the vast valley. Far off, Topanga State Park was burning. Hundreds and hundreds of acres on fire, the smoke visible in the firelight and rising high into the night sky. I could hear people down on the pier below, sudden bursts of laughter and shouts of joy reaching me at the top of the Ferris wheel. The smell of hotdogs and popcorn heavy in the air. No one on the pier seemed alarmed by the fire. Maybe because it was the third fire that year. Maybe because it had been burning for a week and no one really cared anymore, or maybe because it was December and no one believed a fire could be that bad in the winter. The fire lasted another week and was only contained after the winds calmed down. A week after it ended, my father drove me and my younger brother up into the hills to look at the land. The ground was motionless. The oak trees destroyed; their limbs cauterized in place like a kind of black lighting against the blue sky. The land was utterly barren. My father said nothing. He just stared at it for a long, long time and cried.

"Sami," a female voice says. And I think that's the day I lost him. The day he was no longer my father, but a stranger. "Sami," the female voice says again, and I turn away from the window, from the dust storm below. A young secretary is looking at me. She is wearing a white, short-sleeved dress with black polka dots and black high heels. I wonder, only briefly, if my mother would like her dress. Then, I wonder what the secretary feels about her dress, if she feels weak and vulnerable or strong, confident. I wonder what she thinks of my dark, navy-blue, short-sleeved tea dress. A dress my mother would call a "church dress."

"Yes," I say, the image of destroyed oak trees still clear in my mind.

"Thomas is ready for you," she says and leads me into an office. The office is bright with natural light coming in through big windows. A man in his 50s, who I assume is Thomas, is sitting behind a large desk. He's wearing a dark, navy-blue suit.

"Sami, please come in," he says standing up. He walks to me and shakes my hand then motions to one of the chairs in front of his desk. "Have a seat," he says with a smile and walks back to the chair behind his desk and sits down. I briefly look around the office. Covering the wall behind him are black and white photos of films that were made in the 40s and 50s. The photos are behind-the-scenes-shots. I notice he has a few photos of movies that my father produced.

"Thanks for meeting with me ... I'm told you recently finished up filming ... I've seen your work. You have made some excellent documentaries," he pauses briefly. "Small documentaries, but beautiful, nonetheless. Your work on the Southern California orange groves and the development of land here was informative," he says, pausing again. He looks at me for a moment, then, "I love your father's work as well. I guess the apple doesn't fall far from the tree," he says smiling.

"He's helped me out a lot," I say, still thinking of the oak trees. There is a brief pause.

"My assistant filled you in on what we would like you to do?" he asks, but it's not really a question. "I know you're probably busy with postproduction, but have you had a chance to think about the possibility of taking on the project?"

"Yes," I say. "But like I told your assistant, I have never produced a political film before."

He waves this away. "We want someone who has never produced a political documentary before ... your work has a very youthful quality about it ... and we think you can bring that quality to our project."

"Okay," I say. And although I have already decided to take on the project, I still feel a little uneasy, a little unsure of how exactly I can bring a youthful quality to a political film. He seems to sense my hesitation and smiles warmly.

"Well, let me tell you about the project ... maybe that will help you decide one way or the other about taking it on ... our research team says '67 is going to be a very interesting year for the nation ... but especially for California ... planned marches ... demonstrations have been organized for this year as well as large music concerts ... and the majority of these events will be located in and around the Bay Area." He pauses. "We're seeing a kind of pilgrimage of young people from all over the country to

San Francisco. There is a lot of excitement, and the political spirit of the young people has been picking up tremendous speed," he says.

I sit still, listening.

He hesitates just for a moment then continues."We are definitely looking for a specific agenda ... there is a strong desire to promote democratic social programs," he says, looking at me intently.

"Okay ... I think I understand," I say, not understanding at all. "What is the main theme of the film ... do you want me to cover politics in general, or are you looking for something more specific?"

"To be honest, there is a felt need to discuss topics that ... challenge conservativism ... we—myself and the financial backers— are left leaning," he says, warming up now, feeling comfortable. "So protests that get to the heart of socialism will be appropriate ... we want to illustrate topics that highlight the value of socialistic progressivism ... especially as a youth movement." He stops and looks out the window.

I follow his gaze. Studio City sits like a pagan god of hope. In the distance, its suburbs give off a sense of being prearranged, beautiful and green; a mixture of old Spanish bungalows and the West Coast's take on small, humble craftsman bungalows. And for some reason, I am reminded of a movie set.

"Although we have a timeline of events for you to film, if you take on the project, we still want to keep the timeline loose enough for you so that we can set up possible interviews and also so that you can get on film any spur of the moment events that pop up. We already have an agreement with Dr. Miller at U.C. Berkeley for an interview ... he teaches political science. He has strong views on the positive impact of socialism," he pauses. "We have rented a couple of rooms in the Haight-Ashbury district ...

for you and the crew. There is substantial backing to cover the costs for the entire year," he says.

I think about this for a minute. "Is this for theater?" I ask.

"No, it's to be shown in universities across the entire country. Specifically, to political science majors ... our private investors want to influence future leaders," he says.

"And what about the style ... is this a straightforward storyline?"

"Oh, I'm glad you asked that. We want the film shot guerrilla style ... we want the film to feel gritty and unrehearsed. To that end, you'll have a skeleton crew and gear. We'll provide a van for you, the crew, and the equipment."

"What about lighting?" I ask, already knowing the answer.

"We want you to use natural lighting for outside shots and for indoor scenes ... use whatever lighting is available ... we're looking for authenticity," he says.

"What is the pay?" I ask, more out of curiosity than need.

"Room and board, a small per diem for you and the crew, and a small, but still competitive salary for you," he says. "The crew will be paid hourly based on time spent filming."

I nod, but I'm not really worried about it. I live a kind of nomadic existence, floating between film locations, my father's house in L.A., and my mother's house in Palo Alto.

We both sit quietly. He is waiting for me to agree to the project. I try to picture the youth that are wandering toward San Francisco. I think of the pictures in the waiting room of young people protesting the Vietnam War, and a sense of disorientation begins to slowly flow through my mind. There is a kind of beauty to it ... a beauty in which the youth thunder and lament, and I try to see myself in the midst of protests. The effect is dreamlike. I think of the dust storm below. I wonder if it has faded. I think of the burnt oak trees. I think of the philosophy professor at Syracuse. I think of the ideas he explained. Scholasticism. Humanism and Rationalism ... a Rationalism that maneuvers into Romanticism ... and a Romanticism that almost two hundred years after it was born found its expression in the Beatnik movement of the 40s and 50s. The ideas begin to pick up speed, pick up strength: the youth movement. The counterculture. Free speech. Women's lib. Eastern mysticism mixed with atheistic existentialism, pantheism, middle class values, Vietnam, free love ... a kind of display of ideology.

Thomas is looking at me. The large windows rattle. The Santa Ana winds are relentless. I remember the dread I felt while driving, and my thoughts begin to slip. I try to focus, to concentrate, but the ideas blend together in my mind ... key words, important transitions in human thought. I try to recall the flow of thought in the Western tradition, the chronology, the timeline of events ... the machinery of developing ideas. An image of some unstoppable beast flashes through my mind. My thoughts are ... forceful. Words flash before me — a restlessness, a suggestion to my mind, as if the ideas were a living thing that could speak.

"If you agree to take on the project, I can introduce you to the crew," Thomas finally says.

I shake off the emotions with tremendous effort. Thomas is looking at me intently. I stare back. Topanga burns.

"Yes ... I will take on the project," I say, but I don't feel comfortable. I don't really care about politics, and I'm worried I won't have the needed understanding to accomplish what he's wanting.

He nods and picks up the receiver. There is a brief pause as he waits for someone on the other end to answer. Then, "Yeah. Okay."

A minute later, two young men walk into the room. They look at me and smile.

"Sami," Thomas says standing. "Meet Stanley and Leo." I stand up and shake hands with them. My thoughts are still there, still talking, but the volume is turned down now.

"Stanley has extensive experience as a cinematographer and will be working the camera," Thomas says. "Leo will run sound for you." They are maybe a year or two younger than me. Stanley is the taller of the two and has dark brown hair. He's wearing a white t-shirt, blue jeans, and brown boots. Leo, who's a few inches shorter, has blonde hair and is wearing brown bellbottoms and a black-and-brown- striped, button-up shirt.

CHAPTER 4

Two weeks later, I'm driving on Interstate 5 through the San Joaquin Valley. The valley is a vast basin that sits between two mountain ranges and spreads from L.A. in the south to Redding in the North, 545 miles of arid land that is a strange mixture of drought and irrigation, a mostly featureless landscape of hot dry air in which farmers grow 25% of the country's food supply including alfalfa, wheat, pistachios, tomatoes, oranges, walnuts, almonds, grapes, along with millions of cows for milk and beef production. This corridor is only one part of the 5 which runs from the Mexican border all the way up through Oregon and Washington and ends at the Canadian border.

I continue to head north through the valley. I pass large, hand-made signs announcing oranges for sale. An abnormal heat wave has hit the valley. It's almost a hundred degrees as I pull off the 5. I drive east down a dirt road towards Bakersfield. Ten minutes later, I come to the Hermenegildo Garcés Orchard. A faded blue pickup truck sits at the entrance, and in the back of the truck are baskets full of navel oranges that were harvested a little early due to a warm December. A girl is sitting on the back of the truck, her legs hanging over the edge. She looks young, maybe ten. She's wearing dirty jeans with the legs rolled up past her ankles. She has on old Mary Janes and a deeply faded red and white plaid shirt. An older man smoking a cigarette stands beside the truck. I park, get out of the car, and look up into the bright blue sky for a moment. I feel the hot air surround me, suffocating my thoughts. I try to smile.

"Hello," the little girl says.

"Hi," I say and wave a little.

"Do you want some oranges?" she asks.

"Yes, please."

"89 cents for two dozen," the little girl says. She wipes sweat off her forehead. She has light brown hair. The man standing next to her doesn't say anything. He's wearing faded blue jeans, old boots, and a worn button-up shirt that once was blue. He looks at me and adjusts his weathered hat.

"What's your name?" I ask the little girl.

"Kathleen ... but everybody calls me Kat," she says.

"It's nice to meet you, Kat ... I'll take two dozen." Kat slowly puts two dozen oranges into a paper bag, counting to herself as she goes. She hands the bag to me. I give her a dollar.

"Do you want some pips?" she asks me. Before I can answer, she puts her hands in a large basket and shows me the orange seeds.

"Fifty cents a pound," she says. I look down at her small hands holding the dry orange seeds.

"Hold on," I say and walk back to the car. I put the oranges in the back seat and take out a camera. I walk back over to Kat.

"Hold your hands out, please," I say. She lifts her hands up a little higher. I hold the camera up and zoom in on her hands. They are small and delicate, and there is dirt under her fingernails. I take a couple of pictures. There is a quality of the seeds in her little hands that whispers something in my mind. I look out at the immense orchard behind them for a few moments. It's quiet. Something about the man and the little girl reminds me of my own childhood. Reminds me of my relationship with my father. Looking at them, I briefly wonder about the nature of fatherhood and what this life feels like to a dad. I glance at the man standing by the side of the truck then back at Kat. I wonder if they go on walks together.

My father took my little brother and me on walks through the large orange groves of Los Angeles. I loved those walks with him and miss those days. He told us about the history of Los Angeles and the spiritual experience of working the land. He said there was a kind of echo from the Garden of Eden that could be heard by the human soul when laboring and toiling in the soil. He wanted my brother and I to understand something important, something that went deeper than the actual labor.

But I didn't really understand. I was young, and I just wanted to be around my father. I loved being connected to him. I loved when he would see me. Really see me. He taught me to find meaning in the hot Santa Ana winds ... the winds meant something to him. He felt like the winds were a kind of metaphor, but I'm not sure for what. He tried to teach me how to read indications in the fires that tore through Southern California year after year. He tried to point out the important signs that could be inferred from the slow destruction of land once used for agriculture but now turned into suburbs. He taught me to look for meaning in the artistic expression of humanity. I didn't understand then that he was trying to teach me about the beatific vision. I didn't understand that he was losing his mind or that he was trying to teach me about a spiritual reality that transcended the effects of insanity.

He knew I had the same affliction as him before even I knew. He could see certain characteristics, certain rituals in the ways I thought, the ways I behaved. I didn't understand that he was trying to help me to see through the darkness to something beautiful, meaningful.

The doctors put me on lithium. It made my hands shake.

I look down at Kat's hands. An overwhelming urge to call my father, to hear his voice ... to see his face, his smile, collides into me, rushes over me.

CHAPTER 5

I pull into the Haight-Ashbury district a few hours later and look at the brightly-colored houses—blue and purple, yellow and orange, white and pink—as I drive onto Buena Vista Avenue. Most of the houses are Victorian, but the two rooms Thomas has rented for Stanley, Leo, and me are in a large, two-story Spanish house that overlooks Buena Vista Park. I park across the street, smoke a cigarette, and look at the house. The architectural style is in the Mission Revival vein. And for some reason this relieves me, but I'm not sure why, maybe because the style is ... *feels* ... natural to California, not imported like other styles. The front of the house is framed by large, bright-red Bougainvillea that are fully mature. I can hear muffled laughter and music coming from the house. As soon as I register this, a low almost imperceptible anxiety forms in my mind, and I can feel my chest and stomach tighten. I smoke another cigarette, and the urge to call my father washes through me again. I picture his face in my mind, and the anxiety begins to fade out.

I grab the oranges and walk up to the front door. A young woman answers. She has long blonde hair and blue eyes. She's wearing a very short dress.

"There is already enough confusion. And I already told them to stop blending Eastern thought with a political movement," she is saying to someone over her shoulder. She looks at me and smiles, "Sami?" she asks.

"Yes."

"I'm Autumn ... Stanley and Leo are here." She says and gives me a hug. I hand her the oranges. She takes them and motions for me to follow her into the house. I wonder if Autumn is her real name.

The house is beautiful, and Autumn tells me it's almost all still original, except for some of the bedrooms. We walk into the living room. Men and women are sitting in a circle on the floor. The walls have posters on them for concerts and events in San Francisco. The air is permeated with marijuana smoke, and even though it's not really making a difference, someone has lit sage incense. "House of The Rising Sun" is playing on a record player. A young man with a thick, black beard and no shirt is playing the guitar, even though it can barely be heard over the music. Different colored carpets cover the living room floor, and books and records are scattered around the living room.

Autumn is talking to a teenage girl. "Look, I understand," Autumn is saying in a parental tone, "but you still need to be careful; there are a lot of hawks out there. And you, my darling, are a dove." The teenage girl is nodding, but the rest of her body language implies she is not really listening. I pick up a few books: *Naked Lunch* by William S. Burroughs, *On the Road* by Jack Kerouac, *Howl* by Allen Ginsberg, *The Doors of Perception* by Aldous Huxley. I put the books back down.

"Let me show you the backyard," Autumn says. I follow her down a narrow hallway and out the back door. Spanish Mission Red tiles spill out from the backdoor and fan out to the edge of a small but well-manicured, bright green lawn. A very tall hedge completely surrounds the backyard on three sides, giving a feel of privacy. The hedge is groomed, and I wonder who is taking care of the backyard. Large vines of bright yellow Carolina Jasmine climb up the back of the house. Stanley and Leo are sitting on an old wooden bench at the back of the lawn drinking beer and smoking cigarettes.

"Hey Sami," Stanley says. Leo waves. I smile. Autumn sits on Stanley's lap, and this surprises me. They can't have met each other more than a few hours ago. She takes the cigarette out of Stanley's hand and takes a drag and hands it back.

"Autumn," someone is yelling from inside the house, "the guy says he can't do anything until he has—and I'm quoting here— 'visual confirmation.' There is a brief silence, and Autumn sighs and takes Stanley's cigarette and looks out at the yard.

I light a cigarette and sit down on the bench. No one is talking.

"The human tendency toward paranoia is ... exhausting," Autumn says quietly, almost a whisper, and it is clear that she is talking more to herself than to us. Nobody says anything. A few minutes later, Autumn stands up and says to me, "Let me show you your room." The bright orange poppies that someone has planted on either side of the bench ripple in a gentle breeze.

"Sure," I say, standing up. She walks back into the house, and I follow her up the stairs and into the second bedroom. The room is spacious and has hardwood floors. The walls are completely covered in music posters ... some are of concerts and some are album covers. There is a small fireplace in the corner and a small stool made to look like a brightly-colored mushroom.

"It's nice," I say and briefly wonder how she and Thomas know each other. I look at Autumn and smile. She smiles back.

Sometime later, maybe an hour, I'm not really sure, I'm standing in the backyard drinking gin, which I brought with me, and smoking a cigarette. The backyard is still and quiet except for the occasional burst of laughter coming from inside the house. I'm momentarily tempted to go upstairs and take a Nembutal but decide against it. Instead, I finish the cigarette and walk into the living room near the front of the house. About twenty people are sitting around passing joints to each other. Music fills the room. Autumn is sitting on the floor, her eyes closed, head slowly moving forward and backward to the beat of the music.

A young man walks up to me, "I heard you guys are making a film," he says slowly. I look at him carefully and nod. "Cool ... man," he says, looking at me then drifts off toward the kitchen. I notice a young girl smoking a joint. She has light brown hair that is very long and what looks like hazel eyes. She smokes the joint easily, well-practiced, her gaze focused on one of the posters on the wall. She looks so young that I assume she's a runaway. She hands the joint to a slightly older girl sitting next to her. I look back at the young girl, and I wonder where she's from. Maybe the Midwest.

Numerous conversations are going on at once. "It's all there," a young man is saying, "everything you need to know ... transcendentalism ... I'm telling you, Ralph Waldo Emerson and Henry David Thoreau understood, they rejected rationalism ... there is no heaven, there is no hell, everything is divine ... people are basically good ... basically divine ... but they get corrupted by the straight society ... nature will teach us how to embrace our divinity."

Someone else is saying, "Etymology demonstrates subjectivity ... you know? Words have always changed in meaning, that means something ... you know? I mean, if your parents say there is a God, they are meaning something ... a kind of God they

believe in, you know, to them the word means something good …
but if you go back far enough the word God meant other things
… like a kind of *graveyard* … you know … that means something.
There is no absolute truth in language … that's something the
middle-class can't seem to accept."

Someone responds, "Oh man, that's why we keep getting
these plastic hippies showing up, fucking hippie tourists … they
crawl out from their happy, neat middle-class homes after
Sunday church service and walk around like they are hip. That
Rachel who sometimes stays at the house down the street is one
of them—"

"I heard she got strung out on smack," someone else says,
cutting the person off. There is a brief pause, then, "Someone,
I'm not saying who, taught her that she could take the edge off of
meth with smack."

Another pause. "No man, you're thinking of Rebecca, not
Rachel."

"Did you hear the cops busted Augustus's amphetamine lab
in Berkeley?"

"Ah shit, man, that was like two years ago."

And as I head toward the backyard, I pick up other terms,
other words. Key phrases: *through the mind's door. Ascends.
Higher Law. Over-Soul. Unitarianism.*

CHAPTER 6

I stay in San Francisco for a couple of days. But we're not scheduled to start filming for another week, and I need to wrap-up the post production of my documentary about the relationship between theology and the arts, so I drive back to Los Angeles to my father's house.

He's not home. His room looks untouched. I tell myself he's on set somewhere, I'm not really sure where. Maybe Arizona, maybe New Mexico. I'm standing in the backyard staring out at the city below. Heavy gusts are pushing through L.A. I'm watching the palm trees bend in the wind and the water in the swimming pool ripple.

Later that night, I'm mildly drunk and checking that all the windows in the house are locked, and when I walk into my father's bedroom, I notice a bunch of pictures spread out on the bed, pictures my little brother drew when he was three or four. I stare at the pictures for a moment. I pick one up, a picture of a cat in some grass and a rough stick figure of our father. I actually remember the cat. Our father bought it for my little brother a long time ago. "I love cats and daddy," is crudely written at the bottom. Something in me, in my chest, in my mind, begins to crash, and I have to put the picture back on the bed and leave the room.

After checking the windows, I'm standing out back smoking a cigarette and staring out at the vastness of city lights below. A sea of lights. The winds have subsided, allowing a heavy fog to roll in and cover parts of the city.

I'm not sure how long I've been standing out back looking down at the city lights when I slowly register that my mother is talking to me, asking me a question, and I realize I'm back in the living room.

"Did you say yes to the job?" she is asking me over the phone.

"Yes," I say, dimly present. There is a long pause.

"Well ... what is it?" she asks impatiently.

"They want me to make a documentary on the political aspects of the counter-culture movement ... especially as it pertains to socialism."

There is a brief pause. "Are you ... still ... talking to your father?" she asks cautiously. Nervously.

I sigh. She left him when I was 16 after the accidental drowning of my little brother at summer camp. He was 9 years old. She lives in Palo Alto, in a house my father paid for.

"Your hair is too long," my mother tells me over the phone. Then says, as if to herself, "Professional young ladies should have shoulder length hair ... you are starting to look like some of those hippy girls with your hair down to your mid-back."

I don't bother responding. She is always picking apart how I dress, how I look. Instead, I think about the city lights and the fog, and I am reminded of the burning hills I saw all those years ago. I think about the Santa Ana winds driving the flames, the strong winds compelling the fire to greater violence—

"Are you listening to me, Sami?"

"Yes," I say. I can see the bright flames thrashing in the wind.

CHAPTER 7

A week later, I'm standing in an upper room above the Red Dog Saloon in Virginia City, Nevada. We are setting up for an interview with Paul Goodman. The itinerary that Thomas gave me says I'm to interview Goodman about his book, *Growing Up Absurd*. Thomas included a brief summary of the ideas covered in the book and a list of questions to ask.

"Did Thomas explain why we are using a double system for this doc?" Leo asks.

"Sound effects, especially anything that is naturally occurring," I say. "He wants an organic feel ... but with sound that sharply juxtaposes any images we get." I pause here, thinking. "Although there is a specific agenda, he wants the documentary to feel innocent," I say pausing only for a moment, "and there is an expectation of a fair amount of b-roll ... and before you ask, I don't know who they hired for the voice-over."

Leo nods. For some reason, his question about the double system causes indefinable anxiety to cut across my mind.

"Where's the rights bible?" I ask.

Leo is silent for a moment. "I think Stanley has it," he says.

We are both quiet for a minute. Stanley has already set up the camera for the interview.

"Tell Stanley when he gets back that we are ready to go. Mr. Goodman should be here anytime," I say and walk out of the room. I head downstairs into the Saloon. I order a gin and take a Nembutal. The bar is mostly quiet. A band is practicing on the small stage at the back of the room. I remember someone telling me the main singer is Mark Unobsky. I was also told that he is a fairly well-known psychedelic rock and blues musician. I feel indifferent to this information.

I order a second gin and listen to them practice. The reverberations of the guitar sound unnecessarily harsh. A machine-like sound. A sound of devastation. Someone has put up a full-size replica of Pablo Picasso's *Guernica* on one of the walls. The painting is a heavy-handed contrast of black and white and grey colors. The line work of the painting makes everything look jagged ... like I would cut my hand if I were able to touch the images in real life. It all feels frightening, demoralizing. I focus on the mother at the far left of the painting. She is screaming up at the sky. A dead child in her arms.

The Nembutal is beginning to make contact with my brain, and my thoughts begin to slowly drift ... I wonder about the role of art as a political statement ... as an ethical statement, the painters obsessed with capturing dread rather than beauty. Francis Bacon's *Painting 1946* comes to mind. I concentrate on the central aspect of it ... on the man holding an umbrella ... the deep shadow covering part of the man's face ... his eyes are hidden in darkness, but there is an impression that he is staring directly at the viewer. The man has a brutal efficiency that seems unfeeling. Intimidating. There is a profound sense of meaninglessness and ... disorientation.

I look back at the mother holding her dead child.

Twenty minutes later, Paul Goodman is sitting across from me, and I'm asking, "What were you hoping to accomplish with your book *Growing Up Absurd*?"

There is a slight pause as Goodman looks at me. "Did you read it?" he asks.

I pause. "No ... but I read a brief on the ideas that you express in the book," I say, looking at him. He is wearing a collared white shirt, open. No tie. And over this a dark worn-out sweater. His hair is untamed, a mixture of grey and dark brown. He is handsome in an unintentional kind of way ... there is a carelessness about him, an implied abandon.

"Uh ... well ... okay ... I, I, I was attempting to ask why should the young ... why should the delinquents respect the collective standards of American society ... especially when that very society itself does not offer any hope or compassion, you see," he says and stops for a moment. "American society is exceptionally cold and unforgiving. Especially toward young men. The culture demands respect from young men but offers none in return ... even if they obey, you see. This is a strange attitude in one sense, considering that, apparently, something like ninety percent of Americans claim to be Christians. The Bible's position on showing respect to all people, regardless of their behavior or attitude, seems to be in stark contrast to the American attitude that respect is earned, not given. There is no foundation for young delinquents to build on. Poor education, a lack of meaningful work." He stops.

"And it is conservatives that are pushing this agenda of conformity?"

"Yes ... well, no. Maybe. They say they want rugged individualism ... to celebrate the creative individual, but they end up trying to achieve this individualism by demanding conformity to their way of attaining it. And the point of this conformity and individualism is really an attempt to get back to a kind of ... Garden of Eden ... a man-made one, as it were. They believe traditionalism, especially as it pertains to Christianity, will give us a happy life."

The gin and Nembutal are hitting hard now, and I have to make an effort to recall some of the questions that Thomas wanted me to ask. Then, I remember I'm holding a list of questions. I look down at the questions. "So you're saying that America promises young men meaning, value, purpose, but only in exchange for their obedience to conservative values?" I ask.

He looks at me for a moment. "Look, we are talking about American culture today. Here. Now. But the American culture ... our society is nothing more than the latest expression of ideas that go all the way back to the Renaissance, the Enlightenment ... the promotion and celebration of humanism ... as a philosophical approach to life. Christian ideology is very anthropocentric as a result ... this dilutes their theology," he says, smiling softly.

"Of course, my position is also anthropocentric. But I'm starting from Nietzsche's premise, 'God is dead. We have killed him.' Perhaps a better way of saying it ... to a Western mind, is to say that America is nothing more than a modern tower of Babel. It's not that we think God is actually dead or that we somehow killed him. It's simply that we don't believe he even exists in the first place. God, as an idea, is dead. We have destroyed the idea of God ... for the western Christians today, especially in America, faith in God is blind. Without reason, you understand. William James has suggested, as far as I understand, that we should perhaps still hold onto the idea of God, as the idea is still useful, even if the idea is false ... everything else I say from now on is built upon this basic premise. 'God is dead.' We must look to ourselves for meaning," he says and looks at me. "We are a modern tower of Babel."

His words, "we must look to ourselves for meaning," cause me to remember myself at seventeen, driving my father's car through the Hollywood Hills at two in the morning. The Santa Ana winds had been heavy for three days in a row.

I'm not sure why Goodman's statement reminds me of that night, and I'm trying to stay focused, trying to stay present, trying to make an effort to understand the principles underneath the outward issues, attempting to understand the ideological dots he is connecting together, and I'm pretty sure he is saying that humanity, as a philosophy, is like a tower of Babel. Meant to unite people with something other than God. The idea that significance, real meaning, is found in humanistic efforts rather than in religious ones. Ultimately making Christianity dead.

My father would agree—conventional Christianity is hollow. A performance in public respectability, but just that, a performance. He would say that true Christianity is found in outcasts, like the beatniks. The *beaten down ones*. A compassion forms in my mind. I try to envision myself driving the empty roads of the Hollywood Hills—the implications of the empty roads as a house of mourning. The idea that Christ would walk those kind of roads. The feeling of compassion toward those cast into the gutters fills my chest. The house of mourning.

"Are you okay?" Goodman asks me.

I look at him then down at my clipboard.

"And socialism offers a better answer than conservatism to the young?" I ask, ignoring his question to me.

"I suppose that socialism could possibly be seen in the philosophy of Diogenes of Sinope—an ancient Greek philosopher who helped develop cynicism as a philosophical approach to life. Apparently, he took Socrates' asceticism to such an extreme that Plato wrote that he was a 'Socrates gone mad,'" he says with a smile. "Such a colorful turn of phrase. I think socialism can be seen in Diogenes' Cynicism.

"Socialism is trying to get rid of shame in every category. And to what end? Freedom. Autonomy. Self-rule," he pauses. "I'm not a socialist in the current sense of the word, you see. I'm not a ... a ... uh Marxist, you see. My position is simply that I do not believe there is really a, uh, kind of dispassionate truth that we must be chained to. What do I mean?" He asks

The question is not for me. He is talking to himself.

"There is no religious plot—but, but that does not mean we are left without meaning either," he adds quickly as if meeting some objection in his mind, and his eyes look off. I get the impression he is remembering some moment, some memory. "I don't believe the theists are correct in what they say about life, about gods ... but I also don't believe Marxists and what they say about reality ... that a human being is nothing more than a political creature or organism, you see ... a mechanism whose only function is to serve a political idealism. Human beings shouldn't serve ideas. It should be the case that ideas are there to help us break free from social, political, educational ... traditional constraints, uh, limitations—we need educational improvement," he continues, picking up speed, "our educational system ... uh, what do I mean, the education in this country is overly pragmatic, cold ... we need to stop teaching kids to be good ... I'm not talking about a morally pious or virtuous sense of the word *good*, I mean *good* in the sense of obedient citizens, you see ... but the young look around at what they are *told* to respect ... not *taught* to respect—as if obedience, absolute compliance is the result of a loving willingness and as if the ideas to which they owe their allegiance is the result of some kind of free thought discussion, or loving relationship, you see. Our educational system orders them ... and they, the kids, they look at the social, at the political, at the traditions and realize these things destroy the will, destroy creativity ... I ... uh, let me see if I can give an example ... I think it was Hemingway ... let's see if I can remember," he says, smiling self-consciously, "Hemingway said ... concerning the process of creative writing ... which I take to mean creativity in general ... uh, he wrote—'his talent was as natural as the pattern that was made by the dust on a butterfly's wings. At one time he understood it no more than the butterfly did, and he did not know when it was brushed or marred. Later, he became conscious of his damaged wings and of their construction, and he learned to think and could not fly anymore because the love of flight was gone, and he could only remember when it had been effortless.' It's a long quote, but you see, it captures the delicate nature of creativity, so easily destroyed. We need to change our approach to educating the young ... even the language we use destroys human creativity," he says, pausing. He pulls a pipe out of his jacket pocket and lights it.

I can feel my heart rate picking up. I was not expecting him to talk about the power that beauty has to transform the human mind. A beauty that transcends the efforts of politicians and religious people—I remember one of the art professors explaining the dramatic shift in painting that resulted from the Renaissance. A shift that emphasized human autonomy over the idea of some distant heaven and hell. His idea of beauty as a means around the coldness of politics, around the bitter legalism of religion was something I was hoping to discuss in the art documentary.

"The American religious pay lip service to their god, but they resent their god as *God* with a capital 'G' ... their beliefs are really —in practice, you see—a strange kind of atheism. It's an atheism because they don't really want their god to be *God* ... which becomes, in practice, a non-god. That is a kind of atheism. But they couch their atheism amid the pretense of religious devotional language … the function of this god of theirs seems to be no more than a kind of spiritual amulet that they offer their incantations to and expect to receive all they ask for. Their god is little more than a lucky rabbit's foot … the religious in this country really do betray their god with a kiss … but Marxism is no better, you see," he says dragging on his pipe. "Marxism uses language that pretends to care about the individual as an individual but really dehumanizes us, turns us into livestock—scientific language says we are nothing more than intricate biology. Where can the young go, you see? Where can they go? Psychoanalysis seems to only describe all these issues as psychological events, a peculiarity, a strange turn in the broader field of evolution. But what we need is to find meaning. Language seems to fail us here. Are we left with nothing more than a 'leap of faith'? An act of the will? What will the young do? I don't accept there is a spiritual reality behind everything, but we must be more than biology. So, I am required to take a leap—Kierkegaard's leap, but without hoping there is really some god behind the veil," he says.

"I'm aware there is a contradiction here. I'm denying mind-body dualism … uh, cosmological dualism on the one hand and trying to keep it on the other. William James had the same problem, you see. He became suicidal until he finally gave himself over to … to … the existentialist solution of finding meaning … meaning in the deep—almost spiritual sense of the word—by declaring himself free to choose. It was the ability to freely choose that gave him a sense of meaning. Freedom. Autonomy. Even if there is no, uh, theological, uh, design, no big picture, no absolute purpose to our lives … even if we don't actually have souls, no afterlife, no objective meaning to our existence … we can still find meaning in free choice. I am hoping that educational reform will help ease this juxtaposition of meaning and meaninglessness … reform that celebrates youth, creativity, sexual liberation, freedom from traditionalism. We need to embrace naturalism but not let it push us into cold, hard determinism. Even if the idea of *humanness* is nothing more than a cultural idea, we must still live as if our lives have meaning; otherwise, our problems will never end ... it is up to the youth to reject human traditions that claim to care about the individual but really renounce individualism in practice. These traditions are most clearly seen in the American middleclass culture. It is this culture that the youth are rejecting. This is the counterculture, the anti-middleclass culture we are seeing today; you see. This, this, uh ... obviously puts all of us in an inherently unstable position," he says more slowly. "Look, what we're really chasing here, what really matters at the end of the day is to overcome that unbearable isolation ... alienation ... it kills without ever touching the body ... I believe it stems from an abusive educational system."

The interview ends an hour later, and I head to the bar and order a gin. The bar is quiet. The band is gone. I sip the gin and look at the Picasso painting. I look at the mother screaming up at the sky.

CHAPTER 8

My brother was nine when he drowned at the summer camp in Oregon. My mother blamed my father. My father blamed God. They divorced soon afterwards, my mother took the house in Palo Alto. My father kept the house on Angelo Dr., high up in the Beverly Hills. I was sixteen then, and after the numbness went away, I took my brother's favorite stuffed animals from his room and put them on my bed. I would hold them close at night. I would talk with them. Babar the Elephant. Peter Rabbit. Ferdinand the Bull. Their fur soft against my face. Peter Rabbit … his absolute favorite. I would smell the stuffed animal's fur hoping the fragrance of my little brother would come through. A combination of soap and freshly laundered clothes mixed with sweat and the citric scent of orange groves. But it never did.

I would lie awake at night and try to remember how my brother would talk to Peter Rabbit, what he would say to the rabbit, remember him trying to reenact the stories that my father would read to him at night. I would focus and try to remember the sound of my brother laughing and giggling. I would lay my head on the stuffed animals and cry. I would sing songs to them and ask them questions. I believed that I could somehow reach my brother, somehow talk to him through his stuffed animals—as long as I kept the stuffed animals alive, then my brother was not truly dead. Not truly gone.

I started talking to my clothes at this time. Picking out a dress for the day ... I would apologize to the other dresses for not picking them. This seemed like an important gesture, a way of restoring order. Maybe my mother would come back to my father, come back home. But she never did. At seventeen, I started counting ... it was a kind of unction, a ritual that carried the promise of control, of safety, of purpose. My mother would pick me up in L.A. and drive me to the house in Palo Alto. I would count telephone poles along the way. My mouth silently forming the numbers. Images of my brother's body at the bottom of some nameless swimming pool would sometimes gust viciously through my mind, and I would count faster ... in a kind of fervor.

My mother had friends in the athletic department at Stanford and tried to get me into sports. She put me in golf lessons, tennis lessons, swim lessons, horseback riding lessons, gymnastics lessons, but nothing ever stuck. I would quietly leave the practices and wander the Stanford campus for hours.

Lake Lagunita sat at the western edge of the campus. I was trying to catch tadpoles when I first heard the man's voice. It started as mumbling somewhere behind me. I quickly looked around, thinking people were there, but there was no one. I wondered if maybe someone left a radio on, the voices coming to me from some distant point. Then, the man's voice came into my head, "drown yourself," he said.

I ran back to the main campus. Reading the painting from left to right, an incoherence in the colors. The once harmonious tones now discordant: I was standing in the kitchen at my father's house, pouring orange juice into a cup, my mind fixed on some thought, some idea. "Sami," a man said, and the voice only dimly *registered. I felt a soft pull to respond, but my mind was locked in, barely aware of external data. "Sami." The man's voice was calm. I turned around, and my father was looking at me. "You're spilling the juice," he said, his voice full of understanding. I looked back at the container of juice. I had poured out the entire carton. The juice spilled over the edge of the glass and onto the counter and then onto the floor, splattering my shoes.*

CHAPTER 9

I 'm standing high in the Hollywood Hills. Strong winds from the east push through the San Fernando Valley below me. Palm trees bend, their leaves battered, worn-out, the green color blurred by a layer of dust. I look out at the valley below, a massive sprawl of orange plantations. The wind surges through the orchards, sounding like rushing water. I watch as the plantations slowly disintegrate in the strong winds, the valley washed clean from the domination of modern humanity ... unpolluted beaches in the West, large groves of Arroyo Willow trees, the Ballona Wetlands towards the South, the San Bernardino Mountains east of the valley dotted with pines, oaks, and western junipers. And there, just at the base of the mountains is an old monastery.

I walk towards it, and as I get closer, I can see a holy bramble on fire. The pines, oaks, and western junipers are gone, and the San Bernardino Mountains have turned into smaller, barren mountains, their color a light brown. The wind crashes over me, dry, hot. I feel myself trudge into the monastery. On one of the walls is a wood panel, the Christ Pantocrator ... a Byzantine painting from the 6th century. It shows an image of Christ. A halo around his head, the Gospel in his left hand and his right hand held chest high. ICXC. The painting's color is forlorn, affecting a kind of ideological lethargy, its only purpose to state a fact. I look at this Christ. A feeling of indifference sits heavy upon my mind. I feel nothing with this Christ. Nothing. I want to cry. I want to call out to this empty Christ. But there is nothing.

Something distant, quiet … builds in the back of my mind, and I slowly realize I do not know this Byzantine Christ. I do not know this God. I cannot find my father's explanation of the beatific vision here. I want to see Christ, to sense his divinity, but I only see destruction. A Christ in the desert for forties days and night while Jerusalem burns.

The hot winds rush through the broken-down walls of the monastery and slam into me, pushing my hair in all directions. The heat from the wind makes me feel weak. Tired. My legs grow heavy. I want to sit down, but I am being consumed by the dread that the painting causes in me, a dread that this Christ is not a man, does not understand humanity, a distant Christ, a Christ of the heavens but not of flesh and bone, not affected by the gravitational pull, untouched by thirst or hunger.

As I stare at the painting of Christ, I hear what sounds like music. Old music. A lyre, something similar to a trumpet, and another sound like modern bag pipes. I look around but don't see anyone. I walk outside, and the music grows louder. There is a small garden with eucalyptus and sycamore trees next to the monastery. I hear laughter and a woman's voice singing. Her voice is soothing, sedating.

In the thickest part of the small garden are Bacchus and Ariadne. Bacchus is nude, wearing only a crown of ivy. Surrounding him are two cheetahs, a young satyr, maybe Pan, and revelers, and there is a kind of frenzy to the people around him. Bacchus stares at Ariadne in open lust, a kind of psychosis in his eyes. Pear trees, mulberry trees, and apple trees begin to grow and blossom and produce ripe fruit. Grape vines and ivy vines germinate up around the eucalyptus and sycamore trees. The woman sings with rhythmic pressure, drawing out her voice almost to a low moan, and the pulse of the men's dancing swells nearly to violence. A Thyrsus flower springs up around Bacchus. He plucks it, the flower burgeoning and lengthening in his hand, rich golden honey dripping off its tip. There is a kind of liturgy, a sense of ceremony being bred by a mixture of festivity and solemnity, a cognitive worship driven by ecstasy and madness ... worship that has reason and purpose but is utterly insane.

I feel a heat in my stomach, a rush of adrenaline. Blistering winds lash at my face, and I close my eyes. I try to focus on the woman singing ... try to feel the sweetness of her voice, but the wind is unyielding ... eviscerating my strength, my capacity to think, to focus.

Her voice fades away, and when I open my eyes, I see a man standing alone in the distance, isolated. He is facing away from me, staring out at an immense seascape. I slowly realize I know this painting ... *The Monk by the Sea*. Heavy storm clouds sit along the horizon. Remote and monstrous. The man seems so small compared to the enormity of the ocean and the dark horizon, and the winds rush past me toward the man and for a brief moment, the painting moves, the ocean waves agitated by the sweltering winds. I try to concentrate on the man, the sound of the wind. A violent sound. I hear windows rattling. He doesn't move, just stares out at the sea. The windows rattle and rattle and rattle, and I wake up.

The room I'm in is dark, and it takes me a minute to realize I'm in my bedroom at my father's house. I squint at the wall clock my father brought back from England for me. I think it was a present for my 9th birthday. The clock reads 2:33am. I lay still, the dream still lingering in my mind, but only dimly, the sound of driving wind and rattling windows.

When I can't fall back to sleep, I walk out to the backyard. I turn on the pool lights and sit down on the edge of the pool and smoke a cigarette. I look out at the L.A. valley. My father's house has a 180-degree view from downtown L.A. in the East all the way to the Santa Monica Bay in the West. The pool water is pushed around forcefully in the Santa Ana winds. I try to remember how I got from Virginia City to my father's house, but the memory of driving is absent.

I wish I could hear the woman singing, and I remember the way Bacchus stared at Ariadne. I watch the pool water thrash, spilling out over the coping and suddenly realize that Bacchus is nothing more than a representation.

CHAPTER 10

A week later, I'm sitting in Wagner's Beer Hall in San Francisco's North Beach. Stanley and Leo are next to me. It's early afternoon, and the morning fog is finally dissipating. We're supposed to be going over the filming schedule for the day, but none of us seem too interested.

Leo is saying, "Man, I heard this is one of the oldest bars in San Francisco ... from sometime in the 1800s." There is a silence as this sinks in. Stanley, who hasn't said much in the last 30 minutes, is looking at autographed pictures of famous people who have visited the bar over the decades. He pauses at a picture of Janis Joplin. Minutes pass, and no one is saying anything. I light a cigarette and sip my gin.

"I keep thinking sex is a spiritual experience ... like somehow I can reach some kind of meaning or purpose through sex ... but I don't know if I believe that anymore," Stanley says, still looking at the picture of Janis Joplin. Leo and I look at him for a few seconds. I get the impression he is talking more to himself than us. He finishes the rest of his beer and signals the bartender for another one. Leo and I look at him, not really sure what to say.

"No," he says, "I don't think that's right. I don't think it's actually sex ... more like that high from romance, you know?" he says, finally looking at Leo and me. But it's not really a question he wants us to answer. "I remember watching the beach scene in *From Here to Eternity* as a kid ... I've never forgotten it ... I can't stop thinking about it ... Burt Lancaster and Deborah Kerr ... I know it was fiction, but even in that fiction, they seemed so true. So real. So honest, somehow significant. I snuck into the theater. I think I was 11 or 12 at the time. I was just beginning to notice girls. I've always liked movies, but I guess that's true for a lot of people. That scene ... I was absorbed with the bright sunshine, the small waves rushing up on their bodies, crashing into them. Deborah was wearing that dark bathing suit with the deep v-cut down her chest. Her soaking hair ... and wet pale skin. She seemed so feral ... I didn't know about those things at the time ... I didn't understand about adultery ... but even in that moment, in that scene, it turned bad. They were talking about things I didn't really understand. A bastard husband, a miscarriage. I didn't understand until much later. But still, there was that singular moment in the scene when the waves crashed on them, and they were kissing, and she stood up and ran to lay down on her towel. That one singular moment carried a meaning that seemed ... somehow significant. Shit, I knew then I wanted to be a part of films. I wanted to be the one behind the camera." He stops to take a long pull of his beer.

"In college, a female friend of mine—a psychology major—told me I wanted to be a camera man because I was probably a voyeur," he says smiling, but he is looking down at the table. "I tried explaining it to her, but she didn't seem to care." He finishes the rest of his beer and orders another one.

"She didn't seem to care." Those words are what I'm thinking about a couple of hours later as Leo, Stanley, and I setup our gear in Golden Gate Park. The park is massive, something like a thousand acres, stretching over three miles long and half a mile wide. There is a large gathering of young people, academics, Buddhists and musicians—thousands of people. Later, someone, maybe Leo, maybe Thomas, would tell me there were over thirty thousand people at the event.

For some reason, I don't really want to interview people right away. I feel vaguely lethargic, so I send Stanley and Leo out to get b-roll. I light a cigarette and sit on a bench. The air is cool and dry, and I watch the people, some dressed like greasers, some in see-through tops, some shirtless despite the cool weather. I watch a young man blow large soap bubbles into the air.

After a few minutes I walk over to a table where a young woman is selling paintings. Printed replicas. Mostly modern. But I notice she has a replica of Philippe de Champaigne's painting, *Saint Augustine*. I stare at the painting. It reminds me of something my father said about the early Catholic mystics, something about the writing of St. John of the Cross and his poem "Noche Oscura" and St. Teresa of Avila's, "The Way of Perfection," both describing the beatific vision.

"She didn't seem to care … "

For some reason I can't shake these words, the connotations involved, a condition in human nature. Suddenly, I wish I could see my father and think about calling him on a payphone, but I can't remember where he is, maybe on set somewhere. My stomach tightens, and I feel a heaviness slowly form in my mind, almost physical, and I can feel it, actually feel it trickling down into my chest. The desire to call my father, to hear his voice, to walk with him in the orchards is nearly overwhelming. I'm on the verge of crying.

Someone laughs loudly, snapping my mind back to the

present. I blink rapidly, trying to remember what I'm doing here. I look down at the filming agenda for this event. The "Gathering of the Tribes," a scheduled *happening*. I'm supposed to get a lot of b-roll and conduct interviews focusing on socialism, civil rights, and the war in Vietnam. I stare at the list of questions I'm supposed to ask, reading them slowly, my mouth silently forming the words, but there is a disconnect in my mind, and I'm having trouble remembering the point of this event.

Then, the band on stage starts a new song and loud, almost-euphoric cheering sends a physical vibration crashing through the park. The music is loud, and the continuous beat of the drums is soothing. I count the beats, waiting for alleviation from the ever-increasing heaviness in my mind, my chest, my stomach, the feeling of not being able to breathe, and I realize I'm having trouble keeping track of the beats—struggling to keep track of the passing of time. I remember my father telling me about Falret's *folie circulaire*. This seems important, but I can't remember why, and the people are dancing, laughing.

I get up and start walking around. An hour later, maybe two, I'm not really sure, I'm back in the parking lot standing next to the van. I want a drink, but instead, I light a cigarette. Another small group of young guys and girls has formed, and I notice one of the girls, maybe eighteen or nineteen, is holding a bunny rabbit in her lap. I fixate on the rabbit's fur, golden brown mixed with white. Peter Rabbit … my brother's favorite stuffed animal. I stare at the rabbit in the girl's lap. Its long ears and fur have a calming effect on me, and my stomach muscles start to relax.

"Sami," someone says, and I turn away from the rabbit. Stanley and Leo are back. Leo is smoking a cigarette, and his eyes are slightly red and glassy. Stanley is asking, "What are we doing?" I stare vacantly at him for a few seconds.

"Um," I say struggling to bring my mind into focus, "Did you get b-roll?" I finally ask.

Leo smiles at this, and Stanley confirms, "Oh yeah ... it's fucking crazy out there. We got lots of good stuff, including Jefferson Airplane playing on stage, and there are news organizations out there interviewing people—we filmed them doing the interviews," he says, "from a distance so it wouldn't be obvious ... hopefully that shot will demonstrate the kind of widespread interest of the establishment concerning the power of the counterculture movement—oh shit—we even got film of Allen Ginsberg and Timothy Leary ... we couldn't get close, too many people."

I'm nodding my head in approval while drawing in a breath from the cigarette. A few seconds pass, and we are looking at each other when Stanley finally asks, "So ... should we get some interviews?" And I'm actually still nodding, but I'm not sure why. I remember to count the beats of the drummer, but I can't seem to get there, can't seem to keep the rhythm in my head; then, I remember the golden-brown fur of the bunny rabbit, and something like clarity and stillness begin to wash over me.

"Yeah. Okay. Good," I say and stop nodding. "Let's interview those people over there," I say and pause for a moment. "I want to talk to the girl holding the rabbit." Stanley looks at the group I'm pointing to. "But let me go over first and warm them up. I don't want to go in cold," I say, and I start walking away before Stanley can say anything.

I walk up to the group as casually as I can and say hi. They look up at me and smile, a few say hi, and some of the others just wave nonchalantly. There are nine of them, but two of them are kissing heavily, oblivious to anything going on around them. I ask them a few casual questions. Easy "yes" or "no" stuff. They are passing a joint around the group, and a young man takes a long drag and offers me the joint. "Maybe later, thanks," I say, and the joint slowly makes its way around the group. They pass it around the guy and girl who are still kissing.

"I like your bunny rabbit," I say to the young girl, just now noticing we are dressed similarly in high-waisted skirts, although her skirt is long and mine is medium length. She is also wearing a long, flared tunic that is a pretty color of white with blue floral patterns, and I'm wearing a long sleeve blouse with an open collar. Light green. She smiles at me.

After maybe ten minutes of small talk, I finally explain that I am making a documentary on socialistic idealism and ask if they are okay with being filmed. There is a long pause, and my stomach tightens again. I'm pretty sure they think I'm some kind of a narc because I didn't take a drag off the joint, but then the girl with the rabbit, who may or may not be the leader, says, "Cool. Yea."

I wave Stanley and Leo over and introduce them to the group. They give me a thumbs up after setting up, and no one seems to really notice or care. While this is going on I ask the girl her name, not wanting the conversation to cool off. "Meria," she says. The guy next to her hands her a fresh joint, and she takes a small drag off it. Someone else has brought out a bottle of red wine, which is also being passed around.

"Your rabbit has pretty colors," I say. "Does it have a name?"

She smiles and shakes her head. "Names are ownership. We don't own nature. Nature is free. It's our parents who think in terms of owning and exploiting. We are trying to break free from that kind of thinking."

She pauses and someone in the group says, "Right on."

She looks up at me. "We need to return to nature as a way of gaining a kind of purity, a kind of virtuousness. Goodness ... but to exploit nature keeps us from seeing nature as a doorway, a way through." There is a brief pause.

"So, you see nature as a spiritual experience?" I ask.

"Exactly," a young man says and sips from the bottle of wine, "spiritual experience. Man, you need to check out Edgar Cayce ... and Neem Karoli Baba ... they understood." He hands the bottle to the girl sitting next to him.

I need a drink. That's what I'm thinking about when I ask, "What does spiritual experience mean to you?"

Meria smiles, "No one really knows for sure. We are just trying to follow after the poets, the artists ... it starts in nature and then moves us into a deeper connection with other people, and removes division within ourselves, and hopefully an awareness, or experience of a spiritual reality. Just Kierkegaard—"

"But without the Christianity," someone in group says, cutting Meria off.

"I see," I say. "And your parents can't seem to accept or understand that this spiritual journey begins in treating nature with respect?" I ask, watching the bottle of wine make its way around the group.

"Our parents are imposters," someone else in the group says. The conversation is speeding up, and I try to focus.

"They are emotionally cold. My dad threatened to break all my fingers so I couldn't paint anymore," a young male, maybe sixteen or seventeen, says.

"See?" Meria says shaking her head. "Our parents think beauty has no pragmatic value. They see beauty as something like make-believe, like we are nothing more than kids talking to an imaginary friend ... their indifference to nature ripples out, and even the *idea* of beauty carries no value for them."

"We need to be a little sympathetic," a girl says to Meria, "I mean a lot of them went through the Great Depression. The

Second World War. Heavy. Just heavy. There was a lot of prosperity, a lot of innovation. After the war, I mean."

"Yeah, and they got bored," a young man, trying to hold in a breath of marijuana, manages to croak out.

"Absolute imposters. Acting pious."

"Religious fundamentalism," Meria says. "Christians think they own nature."

"Middle class values are a dream," someone else says.

There's a lot of cross talk now, and I've stopped paying attention to who's talking. I just try to keep the theme, the point, in the forefront of my mind.

"Our parents are half-awake, drunk on longing, for a world that could never exist ... "

"Can't the same be said about our generation?" someone in the group asks.

"No," Meria responds. "We hold to deeper beliefs—spirituality has been around for thousands of years ... even if you were to call us bohemians—hedonists, we still are not a modern belief system. Freedom, as a concept, is very old and so is spirituality ... you have the gods of Rome, like Zeus, the Demi-gods of Greece in Olympia, the eastern gods—the Sumerian and Mesopotamian gods, and perhaps even older than these you have Jewish mysticism and the very old nature religions. Our parents are trying to flee the punishment of Adam and Eve, trying to gain back Eden. But we are rejecting this effort ... we are circumnavigating our parent's god. We don't see working the ground in hard labor as punishment ... we don't see nature as an enemy," she pauses as if thinking about something, then smiles. "We see in a mirror, dimly ... but our generation is going to brighten the 'dim mirror,'" she says and winks at me, throwing her head back in bright laughter.

The dim mirror ... the bewilderment of life ... a wasting obscurity found in the mind, and I see Michealangelo's *Creation of Adam*. I see Botticelli's *Venus and Mars*. I see an astronomical event, the North Star and its light is fading, dying. There is a silence and then the supernova and within the supernova a rebirth, a new North Star is being born, and I see this Renaissance, this rebirth in Michealangelo and Botticelli. The rebirth of antiquity, and I watch this new North Star take form, the Age of Reason, the Age of Enlightenment, the modern age and the North Star collapses again, another supernova, building in speed. I feel euphoric, nervous, mesmerized and the ideas born out of this second supernova, ideas born out of human intention ruptures into thousands of little stars and the human mind, that dim mirror, fractures.

And then I'm 10 years old and sitting in stadium seats with my father at the San Luis Obispo County Fair in a tiny town halfway between San Francisco and Los Angeles. We are watching the women's barrel racing event. The announcer is saying something, maybe a name, but his voice is muffled in my ears—I'm transfixed by the women's brightly-colored, long-sleeved button-up shirts and long point collars—some wear deep blue, or yellow, or white. Some have bright sequins along the collar bone and chest of the shirt, intensifying the color. Their decorative belt buckles— brightly polished silver against dark denim—produce in my mind the idea of stars in the night. Some wear their hair in ponytails; most wear it down with a cowboy hat pulled low over their foreheads. They are so beautiful, poised, the clothes accentuating their bodies, their form and the crowd suddenly seems louder, and my face is warm, almost hot, and I want to be like them. It feels like nothing in the world can touch them, that they are brave and strong. As they sit tall on the Quarter Horses.

That night, a feeling of fearlessness begins to grow inside me. I dream of sapphire. The smell of freshly-plowed dirt laced with the slight smell of horse urine blends with the smell of manure, and I see from a great distance, a throne made of deep blue, and around and above and below the throne are many people and angels and there is no sound and everyone is still. I thought it might be a painting, but then the people moved and I knew it wasn't a painting but a real moment with real people, and even the sky around the throne is blue and seems to be alive and I can smell the perspiration of the horses and the people in crowds in the hot noonday sun, and there is a woman with black hair and a black cowboy hat and a bright blue shirt, and there is a unexpected stillness in the horse and the crowd, a momentary inhale and I can't hear the crowd, she has complete control of the animal, and the horse seems to sense the crowd's excitement, eager to start the race, then the noise of the crowd rushes in, suddenly the horse charges out, its body galloping in full strides towards the first barrel, the power of the horse reaching speeds past 30 miles an hour, the woman leaning deeply forward on the horse as they round the first barrel, her cowboy hat flies off, her black hair whipping across her face, and she looks untamed, undomesticated, free in this single moment in time, I want to be like her, to feel the rush of going fast, to feel the Santa Ana winds wash over me. My father is explaining to me, "The daughters of Eve have become as God to the son's Adam," he says. "Ever since that hour long ago. California Holly. Was it really the euphoria of that plant—a kind of symbol, a kind of idea. Her fruit, like tiny red apples, rests among thorny leaves. Hollywood was turned into a temple that covers the whole world. Not even that son of David, walking in wisdom, contemplating his luxurious gardens could understand these matters. This endless toiling. Our parents were anthropocentric in their ideology; they gave birth to affliction. They worship eudaimonism...scientific skepticism. They were looking for a unifying idea. That poet...it cannot hold. 'The center cannot hold,'" and he begins to cry, quietly, and barely above a whisper, "The Kingdom of heaven has suffered violence, and the violent take it by force," he says, looking at me, but he doesn't really see me, he is looking through me, past me, to that kingdom of heaven, "To what can I compare this generation?" he says to himself. "They are like children sitting in the marketplaces and calling out to others, 'We played the flute for you, and you did not dance; we sang a dirge, and you did not mourn.'" He slowly melts away before me. I stretch out my hand to grab him ... I can feel myself looking for my mother and father, but there is only vapor, my hand grasped upon nothing, I'm walking down Market St., and fog is rolling into the city and I stop and stare at the fog, a vague feeling of apprehension, and I can hear mumbling, voices talking in whispers and as I continue walking down the street I notice an ad covering one entire side of 6-story building promising release from boredom if you buy a Dodge Polara and in 3-foot letters someone has spray painted across the billboard, "Welcome To The New Garden Of Eden," and my father and I are walking barefoot through the orchards of the San Fernando Valley, and the sky is clear and blue; the sun warming the pacific, a heavy breeze rushes down the Transverse Ranges and washes over the orchards, making a sound like rushing water in the orange trees, some indication in that sound of wind, "Can you hear it?" I want to ask my father, but he is walking a few feet in front of me, and I almost reach out for his hand, a sense of needing him to protect me, and I hear the voices mumbling, male voices, and my father is drinking, even though he promised to stop, and I see a dark shadow of a man standing in the orchard, and the joy of the whiskey's first glow is on my father and he is laughing and talking to the orange trees, utterly oblivious to my presence, "The center cannot hold" he says over and over, and the breeze turns into a strong wind, hot, the orchards slowly fade away, changing into streets of track housing. There is a smell of smoke, and behind me is a sound, consuming, devouring, speeding toward us. I turn to look and a vast fire is rushing toward us, eating up the orange trees and houses. I scream.

I'm sitting up in bed, sweat dripping down my face. It's four in the morning. I'm in my bedroom at my father's house. I slowly realize I'm clutching the Peter Rabbit stuffed animal. I stare at it for a few seconds, and then, I start crying and am not able to stop.

CHAPTER 11

We went to Disneyland a week after it opened. It was July, and the heat was tiring. I was fifteen, and we were all together, my brother, my father, my mother. We ate cotton candy and walked through Main Street, USA, and the themed lands: Tomorrowland, Fantasyland, Adventureland, and Frontierland.

My mother was listening to a lot of Billie Holiday back then. She would sit out on the back patio looking out at the San Fernando Valley below and play the vinyl record over and over, and I remember Billie's voice having an undercurrent, a sort of longing. My father was always somewhere on set. I watched Lauren Bacall and Humphrey Bogart on TV. Warm winds from the Pacific would sometimes rush up the Santa Monica Mountains, conveying an unease in my mind, even then, even in the happiness of Disneyland and family—the winds produced a feeling of uncertainty, a glimpse—whispering of things adults wouldn't tell you as a child. It was the last year we were all together as a family.

CHAPTER 12

I'm driving back to my father's house from a beauty salon in Century City. I reflexively touch my hair and look at it in the rearview mirror. It comes down just past my ears ... a vague sense of regret.

CHAPTER 13

"You've been gone for three days," Stanley says as he exhales marijuana smoke. We're standing in the backyard of the house on Buena Vista Avenue, and I'm sipping a small glass of gin and smoking a cigarette. There are a lot of random people walking around, going in and out of the house, asking questions like, "You hungry?" "Does anyone have anything?" "Did you ever find Jim?" "Jim was arrested in a drug bust." "I heard he's up north." "Who has the mescaline?" It's noisy, and it takes a few seconds for Stanley's words to register.

"What are you talking about?" I ask. There is a brief pause.

"You walked off in the middle of the interview with Meria ... and you've been gone for three days." Another pause. "Fucking wild, man ... where did you go?" he asks and takes another small hit off the joint.

I sip the gin, trying to understand what he is talking about. Three days.

"Leo thinks you were on an acid trip," he says, looking at me briefly. "You got a haircut ... looks good." I attempt to smile, but there are too many people here, and a feeling of nausea is creeping into my stomach, and I realize I don't actually want to stay in this house anymore. I call my mother and ask if I can stay at her house in Palo Alto.

"Of course," she says, "but you'll be here alone."

"Why?"

"Because I'm leaving for Spain in two days … so you will be here alone."

"Oh … how long are you staying in Spain?"

"A month." There is a brief silence. "Did you get your hair cut yet?"

I pack up my stuff and drive to Palo Alto without letting Leo or Stanley know. I tell myself It doesn't really matter where I sleep; it won't be a problem for the documentary. Palo Alto is only 45 minutes from San Francisco.

CHAPTER 14

"I want to walk around parts of the city and get some shots for scope ... depth ... atmosphere," I say to Stanley.

"I hear the Castro neighborhood is good," Stanley says.

"Okay, I'll get Leo. Meet me out front," I say and walk to Leo's room. He's not there, so I walk out to the backyard. He is talking with a young girl and smoking a joint.

"We're going to the Castro," I say. He nods, blowing out smoke. Thirty minutes later, we find parking on Collingwood Street. We walk down to Castro and 18th. Young men and women dressed in brightly-colored shirts and pants crowd both sides of the street, mingling with older men dressed in single-colored business suits.

"I want a sequence shot—take in everything," I say to Leo and Stanley and wonder if this is what Athens looked like in Socrates' day. If young people, drinking wine, gathered around Socrates and argued about ethics, politics, art, poetry, and the soul. Maybe a young Plato, still drunk from a symposium the night before, is close to Socrates, listening carefully, the very first indications of the Forms developing in his mind. I wonder if Plato convinced the younger generation of a spirit realm with his cave analogy. I can hear the sounds of the Lyre moving their young souls, causing them to think about a higher spiritual reality. An abstract reality of the Forms. I wonder if the youth of that day ever felt lost in the wilderness of Athens.

"Hey," Leo says to me. I stop staring at the people walking by and look at him. He's smiling. "You gotta meet this old man. He's 80 years old, and he was actually born here in San Francisco in 1887!"

I stare a Leo for a second, letting his words draw me back into the moment. He's pointing at an old man sitting on some steps in front of a house. There is a small tabby kitten sleeping in the old man's lap.

We all walk over to him. His head is hanging down, resting. The kitten doesn't stir.

I study him for a brief moment before saying, "Hi." He looks up at me and smiles, no lower front teeth. Deep crow's feet around his eyes. He has a long messy white beard. I look down at his hands, a rich black, cracked, a lifetime of labor.

Leo and Stanley give me a thumbs up that they're ready.

"What is your name?" I ask. There is a brief pause.

"Jerome," he says. His voice is raspy.

"Have you lived here your whole life?" I ask.

He nods.

I whisper to Stanley to get a close up of the kitten and Jerome's hands and face.

"My whole life ... lived through the 1906 earthquake," he says. "Had to live in one of the tent cities for a couple of months ... until new housing could be built."

"Tell her what you were telling me about Castro Street," Leo says.

Jerome nods his head, "The Castro is different today ... the whole city is different. I remember when this street was filled with horses and carriages. "

I take this in. I try to imagine what Castro looked like before cars.

"The gold changed everything," the old man says, his eyes drifting a little. There is a brief pause.

"What do you think of this youth movement in the city?" I ask.

He smiles brightly, his soft raspy voice turning to laughter in his mouth. "San Francisco is my daughter," he says. "She has always been reckless. She is taken with paganism ... she longs after Ochosi. She has always desired the kind of truth that is found in the old beliefs," he says, his eyes drifting again. "But she is in love with danger, Grootslang, Inkanyamba ... she tells me she's in love with an Adze. She swoons with the heady desire of mystical experience. She desires to look upon the faces of the gods. She doesn't seem to understand how dangerous ... a longing for ... to see, to really see the gods ... the young will see visions and the old will have dreams." He looks at me for a moment and then past me.

I don't say anything.

His head slowly drifts back down.

"Should we leave him be now," Stanley whispers to me. I look down at the kitten in his lap. The busy sounds of the street rush into my mind. I nod. "Let him sleep," I say, then more quietly, "Goodbye, Jerome."

We walk around for an hour, filming and doing a few short interviews, and I notice a young girl sitting on the sidewalk, smoking a cigarette, her back up against the Castro Theater. A young man is sleeping next to her. He is wrapped in a blanket. The girl is holding a dirty paper cup, weakly attempting to collect donations. Stanley is filming the façade of the Castro Theater; I call him and Leo over and motion to the girl. I get two bucks off each of them and add a five to the bills.

"Hi," I say to the girl, dropping the money into her cup. She looks up at me.

"Thank you," she says and notices Stanley and Leo.

"Would you mind if I asked you a few questions on camera?" I ask.

"No," she says.

"What's your name?" I ask.

She looks a little hesitant. "Is this going on the news?"

"No, we're making a documentary."

"Oh," she says. "My name is Ann."

"Where are you from?" I ask.

"Wisconsin."

"How old are you?"

"Fifteen," she says. There is a brief silence as I attempt to let this settle in my mind.

"How did you get out to California?"

"We hitch-hiked."

"What's his name?" I ask pointing to the young man. More hesitation.

"I don't think he'd want me giving out information like that," she says.

I nod understandingly.

"Why are you here?" I ask.

"This is where it's all happening ... the people are laidback out here."

"Where are your parents?"

"Who cares ... they are uptight, they are oppressive and brainwashed by strict rules," she says, and I'm almost certain she is just repeating what she heard someone else say.

"Do you have somewhere to stay at night?" I ask.

She shakes her head.

"How long have you been in San Francisco?"

"Almost three months."

"Have you been living on the streets this whole time?" I ask, but the question feels insincere, and at first, I am having difficulty understanding why. Then, I realize I would rather talk with Jerome. Someone who has lived a long life and can see beyond the afflictions of this generation. I need a drink.

"Yes ... but we don't mind ... it's better than being back home," she says. The young man next to her is still sleeping, and I wonder if he's passed out from drugs.

"His dad used to beat him," she says briefly looking at the young man.

"My parents didn't do anything like that to me. I used to look to my mother and my father for truth," Ann says and takes a breath. "But they say one thing and live another ... they live lies ... my 9th grade English teacher gave me a Jean-Paul Sartre book. I learned that existence is prior to essence. That's what we are looking for ... or at least I am. I think my friend just wants to get away from his dad ... I am just trying to live authentically ... that's what I'm looking for—to live authentically."

I stare at her briefly. I have the impression, again, that she doesn't really understand what she is saying, that she is just repeating what she's read.

CHAPTER 15

Two days later, we are in Berkeley filming an antiwar protest. There are thousands of people on the Berkeley campus, spilling out onto Oxford Street, slowly marching toward the Army Induction Center. We've been interviewing people for a few of hours, and I feel like we've gotten good footage. I'm asking a Vietnam vet, "Why are you protesting the war?"

He's in a wheelchair, missing one leg. "We are doves, man. Doves," he says. "We want peace, but the hawks want war. They don't know, they don't know what they are talking about … They don't understand what is happening."

"What is happening?" I ask. Stanley backs up a few feet so he can film the young man's entire body, not just his face.

"Our government says this war is about stopping communism … and maybe it started that way, but now it's a dirty war. A fucking dirty war." He is on the verge of tears.

"What do you mean … what's a dirty war?" I ask, focusing on his face then his hands, which are trembling.

"War crimes, killing farmers execution style—violence against non-combatant civilians, burning property, raping women and children, torture, maiming," he says, again on the verge of tears.

"How can you kill a husband—a father, and gang rape his wife and daughter? Where is stopping communism in that? Psychologically, we were devastated ... and for what? The Vietnamese don't even want us there. Our fucking parent's generation went through the great depression and fought in World War II ... they have a different ideology than we do. I guess their ideology is somewhat understandable, but their morality is too tight, they hold on too tightly. They are stubborn. We stand for a different morality than theirs. Obviously, in principle, some of their ideas overlap with ours, but still ... I don't really understand it. I feel like we were taught to fear communism because of what it could possibly produce ... loss of freedom, loss of individual identity, totalitarianism. I was told that at the age of eighteen I owed my country. I had to fight for my country and democracy."

Violent images fill my mind. I can feel the heat of the sun radiating off the Vietnamese land. I can smell the sweat of villagers as they are rounded up. Fear washes through me, spilling out into every corner of mind and body. I try to ignore the images; I try to ignore the intense anxiety. I light a cigarette and attempt to turn my mind to the concepts he is talking about. Loss of identity. A morality that seems more driven by a cold heart than actual warmth, actual kindness. I'm trying to put myself in his mindset of political ideology, but what I actually see in my mind is a different kind of destruction of the land. Instead of suburbs, it's bombs. I look at the young man. I look at his hands. Trembling. I wonder if his hands ever worked the land. I remember Kat's hands.

And I realize I've been quiet too long and blurt out, "Do you feel disenfranchised?" But I'm not really thinking about the question; I'm thinking about a book I saw my father read often, *A Discourse on Meekness and Quietness of Spirit* by Matthew Henry. He would sometimes just read the same paragraph over and over.

"I ... we ... don't *feel* disenfranchised; we *are* disenfranchised," the young man says. And I remember my father saying the book was written in the 1600s—

"The Republicans don't respect us, don't respect our ideas. Our parents dismiss our laments as nothing more than a passing whim. They ridicule us. Call us panty waists," he says, lighting a cigarette. "Did you listen to Reagan's 'Morality Gap' speech last year?"

"No," I say. He reaches into one of his pockets and pulls out a beaten-up pamphlet and hands it to me. It's a transcript of the speech. And although I don't really want to look at it, I can tell he wants me to read it. I read the first two paragraphs to myself, "There has been a leadership gap and a morality and decency gap at the University of California at Berkeley where a small minority of beatniks, radicals and filthy speech advocates have brought such shame to and such a loss of confidence in a great University that applications for enrollment were down 21% and are expected to decline even further. You have read about the report of the Senate Subcommittee on Un-American Activities-it charges that the campus has become a rallying point for Communists and a center of sexual misconduct. Some incidents in this report are so bad, so contrary to our standards of decent human behavior that I cannot recite them to you in detail."

I look back at the young man.

"Can I keep this?" I ask.

"Sure, I've got plenty back at my place ... that guy is all show and no go," he says pointing to the pamphlet. There is a long pause.

"Did you personally see war crimes?" Stanley asks. Something within me collapses. I'm tempted to glare at Stanley. I wish he didn't ask that question. My mind can only handle so much imagery of the destruction that men afflict upon the land, upon each other.

"I didn't see them personally ... but we came across dead villagers where the women were stripped naked—they had been stabbed or shot. I can still smell burning flesh," he says. "I had a buddy in a Special Forces unit ... he saw some crazy shit. You need to understand ... that environment is challenging. It's often hot and muggy ... getting ambushed with guerilla tactics ... that shit creates paranoia, anger, a desire for revenge. Combine that with poor sleep ... and throw in drugs and alcohol ... shit goes sideways quick. There was no real oversight in his unit. Everything is about high body count. Free fire ... no need for proper engagement protocols. Shoot anything that moves." He pauses for a moment.

"I should be careful here, I'm not saying that every American soldier is like that ... and the Vietcong can also be vicious, even to their own people—the people they claim to care about," he says and lights another cigarette. He starts talking about Just War Theory and the emptiness behind the words, behind the ideology.

I don't say anything. I let him take a few minutes. I light up a cigarette. My lower back is hurting from being on my feet for hours. I don't want to press him, but I need to sit down soon. I need a drink.

"Do you think the war is making a difference?" I ask.

"Making a difference? Are you fucking joking? This war is the result of America's best efforts to deal with its own fears, its anger, its hangups ... do you know that the military leadership counts every found rifle of the enemy as a dead enemy? The assumptions made by our side are absurd to a level that is borderline delusional. They are trying to sell this war ... let me ask you a fucking question: if we win this war, then what happens?

Where is the United States actually going? Are we going to be a better place to live? People are people. You can have all the ideology you want, and people will always be people." He pauses for a minute as though gathering his thoughts. "We were told to never question authority—the schools, the priests, the parents, the police—never question authority ... we practiced 'duck and cover' drills in school in case of a nuclear attack," he says. "I lost a leg ... I don't know why ... for what purpose was that necessary ... this life is filled with futility."

I'm looking down at his trembling hands. And for a brief moment I want to take his hands in mine. I want to tell him it's going to be okay. But instead, I light another cigarette and thank him for his time and watch him disappear back into the crowd. I remember sometimes seeing my father sitting on the couch, reading out loud, as if saying the words out loud would somehow give him something to stand on. A truth that could not be destroyed by the indifference of humanity. I can see my father sitting on the couch, reading out loud, "Heaven, for certain, is a quiet place, and none are fit for it but quiet people. The heavenly land of peace, would be no heaven to those that delight in war; turbulent and unquiet people would be out of their element."

As we pack up to leave I start counting in my mind. One, two, three, four, five—

CHAPTER 16

I t's one in the morning, and I'm sitting alone in the backyard of the house on Buena Vista Avenue. I took a couple Nembutal earlier in the evening and decided against trying to drive to my mother's house. My old room is taken, but Autumn said I could sleep with her in her room. I've been sipping gin all night. But despite the Nembutal and gin, my energy is still really high. It was a busy day of filming, and I feel good. I'm going over different camera angles I can use to add a little more creativity to the documentary when Socrates walks into the backyard and stops in front of me. He is wearing blue jeans and a white t-shirt and is barefoot. He looks down at me for a brief moment then beckons me to follow him. I light a cigarette and start following him.

"Where are we going?" I ask him. He doesn't answer me and pretty soon we are walking down Castro St. The fog is thick and the city lights are bright. Neon colors permeate the fog, and I start laughing with the excitement of walking down the streets of San Francisico with Socrates. He starts calling out about the soul, divine signs and dreams—visions granted from oracles. A young woman high on LSD smiles brightly in his face and tells him to stop fretting about religion and philosophy and just let go and stand quietly before oblivion.

Socrates looks at her but doesn't say anything, and we walk further down the street, and the sidewalk blends seamlessly into a pathway leading through thick green trees ... an ancient forest. A rush of emotional delight, a kind of tickle in my mind floods in, and I laugh in pleasure.There is an opening in the woods where tree nymphs and anxious-looking young men and women are sitting around. Dionysus is there, and he starts playing music on a flute. Suddenly, young men and women are drinking wine and dancing, their fears disappearing, the philosophical confusion unable to overcome the music, the mind momentarily rejecting horror and apprehension. There is a profound idea of sexual frenzy in the music. Dionysus plays the flute with greater intensity, and the youth of an entire generation—on the brink of madness—dance and laugh, sweat dripping down their foreheads. The young men laugh, and the young women sigh, drunk on wine, on pleasure, on embracing the sweet torment of emptiness.

Young woman: "Why are you weeping?"

Socrates: "It is better to go to the house of mourning than to go to the house of feasting."

Young woman: "Life is pettiness ... come wise Socrates ... drink deeply with us. Dance with us. Let your eyes rest upon devastating beauty. Taste the obscurity ... the universe is reaching its dusk. Existence precedes essence ... we make our own meaning."

Socrates: "There is a kind of opaqueness ... Delphic pronouncements of obscurity ... can you feel it ... this is oppression."

Young woman: "We would rather be oppressed in debauchery and eat and drink than starve to death in the wilderness of ethical virtue. Drink, Socrates. Drink and dance and kiss a woman, touch her … let your troubling thoughts find rest. Drink and create your own significance."

I watch Socrates stare at the woman for what feels like a long time. She takes his hand and begins leading him away. He looks back at me, motioning me to stay where I am. And as he walks further and further into the woods, I suddenly realize I not in the backyard anymore. I'm standing alone on a street. The feeling of disorientation—lightheadedness, fills my mind. I look around and recognize some of the shops. I've walked five blocks from the house. I think about this for a moment and can't help but laugh.

Thirty minutes later, I wake up Stanley and Leo. I tell him to get their gear.

"What time is it?" Leo asks, his eyes slightly unfocused.

"It's early … about 3 A.M.," I say.

We end up walking the red-light district on Broadway. The bright neon lights are slightly diffused by the nighttime fog, an out-of-focus effect that is mirrored in the wetness of the streets. We move across the street in order to get a wide shot of the neon lights.

"Do you hear that?" Leo asks, removing his headphones. We stand still, listening. Someone is practicing the violin. The sound is small, quiet. I light a cigarette, listening carefully. Every once in a while, the figure of a man walking down the street will appear in the fog and then disappear, and I briefly wonder if one of the figures could be Socrates. Walking the red-light district. Alone.

The sound of the violin—though not being played by an experienced hand still sounds melodious, lonely.

"Yes, I hear it," I say. We stand there, listening. The neon lights coloring the fog and the sidewalk and street in an almost water-color effect of yellow, red, blue, and purple.

CHAPTER 17

I was nineteen and had been staying at my mother's house for the summer. We were sitting in the backyard. She was smoking a cigarette and sipping from a glass of gin. Around her were old photographs of my father and her. Not photographs of all of us as a family, just photographs of her and my father.

"Do you remember the saloon on the backlot of the studio your father worked for?" she asked me.

I didn't say anything.

"The set was a small, western town," she said. "The construction crews turned it into a drinking spot for when they got off work. The town only had one street. Your father spent a lot of his free time there," she pauses, trying to remember something, "You were eight or nine when he started bringing you along." She sips the gin. "I didn't like that he brought you there. We fought about it ... I think he was hoping to teach you about the people who worked hard to make the sets look real. Some of them worked in the orange groves before getting hired to help build sets," she says and looks away.

I have a few clear memories of the set. It was there that I first heard Billie Holiday singing on the radio. Her voice baptized me into a world I knew nothing about, a world that had an appearance of efficacy but was excessive and made men forget the beauty of the land. It had become a source, a matter of production value.

I remember not understanding how my father, a film producer, fit in with the rough men who tended to the construction. Men who earned their dinner in the punishment of Adam; men who lived by the sweat of their brow.

I remember my father getting drunk and telling anyone who would listen that the concepts of particular films were an attempt to put freedom and meaning back into the numbing grind of everyday life, an attempt to escape the sense of futility of work ... to return to a simpler time of harmony with nature. He would talk about The Wizard of Oz—the idea of a land that could be called home. He would talk about the themes in Gone with the Wind, especially the importance of the land. He would talk about the ballad "Somewhere Over the Rainbow." He'd once asked Yip Harburg if "Somewhere Over the Rainbow" was really a song about the land of Jerusalem. My father never told me if Harburg responded.

Sometimes, he would quote T.S. Eliot or preach about the themes of Steinbeck. Sometimes, he would cry; sometimes, he would just stare out the saloon doors. The men would listen to him, probably because he was the producer, but they really didn't seem to care. I remember flushing with anger when they acted indifferent to my father. "Tis no great matter," they would say to him.

Sometimes, after the drink had set in, my father would quietly sing, "There's a land that I heard of ... once in lullaby."

Some days, the Santa Ana's would blow hot, and it would be just me and my father in the make-shift saloon.

"He had a sense of hope back then," my mother told me. "If

your brother didn't drown," she said finally, looking out at the Santa Cruz mountains, "we might still be together."

I got up and walked away because I knew she blamed my father for my brother's drowning. He had no control over the accident. Yet, she blamed him and left him.

CHAPTER 18

I 'm sitting in a lounge chair next to the pool in my mother's backyard. It's sunny, and the late afternoon air is warm against my skin. An occasional soft breeze comes down from the Santa Cruz Mountains, rippling the blue pool water. I've been sipping gin, chain smoking, and reading "The Chrysanthemums," over and over for the last two hours. I think about Elisa, the central character in the short story. I try to picture her in my mind; I try to imagine how I would feel if I were standing next to her as she works the ground, tending the flowers. I briefly wonder if she would like me. A vague anxiety passes through me as I watch a traveling repairman drive his wagon up the road to her house. They talk, and after a little while he leaves, but before he rides off, she hands him some chrysanthemum shoots potted in moist sand.

There's a tremor in her hands, a sense of vulnerability as she gives the chrysanthemums to the traveling repairman. The shoots are small and delicate and seem to indicate something. A kind of intimacy. The bearded repairman takes them and thanks her.

Then later, after the repairman has driven away in his wagon, we are sitting next to each other as her husband drives us into town. She is looking ahead and notices something on the side of the road. And as we get closer, she recognizes what it is. The chrysanthemum shoots. The repairman tossed them to the side of the road. She stares at them as we drive past. She begins to cry quietly, not letting her husband see. I feel a strong longing for connection, mixed with futility. Even the promises of spiritual experience from working the land feel empty. I think of King Solomon and all the ways he tried to find meaning in this life.

I walk inside to refill my glass but decide to just take the bottle out back with me. On the way out, I pick up a coffee table book. It was a gift from someone to my mother. She's had it for a few years, but it looks brand new. Untouched.

The photos are all nature shots. Some animals. No people. I flip to a chapter on roads. The roads are long, sometimes straight, sometimes curving out of view in the distance. Some of the roads are made of dirt, and some are made of asphalt. I stare at a picture of a dirt road running through wide open fields. Cultivated fields. I wonder if this road is similar to the road Elisa and her husband are on, and for some reason, I think about Andrew Wyeth's painting, "Christina's World." Christina is wearing a plain dress. Her face is turned away; she is looking up at a farmhouse in the distance. She is unable to walk. Polio. The setting is rural, and there is no one else in the painting. No one waiting for her, no one to help her. I watch her as she attempts to crawl through a field toward the farmhouse. I wonder if Elisa and Christina would have been friends. I stare at the picture of the road, and I can hear what sounds like people mumbling. Male voices. I look around to see if there are neighbors nearby, but I can't see anyone, and then I wonder if I turned on a radio and just forgot about it, and then, I remember my mother doesn't own a radio. I light a cigarette and down the gin and pour another. I try to ignore the voices, but it's difficult.

There is a disconnect in my mind. Someone is saying my name. I try to concentrate on the documentary, concentrate on the philosophical ideology of the youth movement. I hear myself answering whoever is saying my name, but nothing is registering, nothing is present before me, nothing but the mumbling voices.

"Sami," someone says.

"He threw her flowers away. He threw them to the side of the road," I say.

"Sami."

"I need to show you the painting, the picture of the road I was looking at ... you would see, you would hear ... the futility. The absolute futility ... Luis de Morales' *Man of Sorrows* ... there is no glory, no divine agony, just a human Christ in lament."

"Sami ... "

"I can see him sometimes, the man, I sometimes see him in the corner of a room—and the bunny rabbit with its paw in a trap."

"Sami, it's one in the morning here," my mother says. Her voice is groggy.

"Cut your throat with a knife," a man's voice whispers. I look around; no one is there.

"I miss my brother ... I sometimes have nightmares about drowning—the waters of Meribah," I say.

"Sami."

"God tested us with the waters of Meribah ... urine mixed with semen."

I look at the photography of the road. I imagine myself driving down it. I can see the young flowers lying on the side of the road. Dying.

CHAPTER 19

It's 7:00 P.M., and I'm standing on the front steps of a large Tudor-style house on the Stanford campus. I don't have much energy, and I don't really want to be here, but we're scheduled to interview Dr. Miller, a political science professor, at his office on the Berkeley campus later in the week, and when I called him to set up the interview, he invited all three of us to a small dinner party. "This way we can get to know each other in an ... *informal* setting — life should have something else in it besides protesting," he said.

I smoke a cigarette and stare at the front door. I can hear the faint sound of music and people talking. The sounds cause an unease to bloom in my mind, a sense that I don't belong at this dinner party. I don't fit in with these people, and I almost get back in my car and drive away. I briefly imagine myself driving back to my mother's house, sitting in the backyard, drinking gin. I can see the lighted pool, a calming blue color. I can see the night sky above, filled with stars.

I ring the doorbell, and a Catholic priest wearing a long black cassock with a white collar answers the door.

"Sami," he asks, and before I can say anything, he continues, "I'm Father Lopez—Stanley told me you have short auburn hair."

There are about twenty people standing around in groups of two or three. Stanley is talking with a woman, and Leo is standing by the bar smoking a cigarette, his head keeping time slightly with a song on a record player. Father Lopez hands me a glass of wine and starts to introduce me to everyone—mostly academics at Stanford.

Dr. Miller walks up. "Sami," he says and shakes my hand. "I'm excited to meet you—I very excited by the project you are working on. Hopefully, some good will come from it." He pauses. "Thomas is interesting. I don't know if I've ever known a political ... uh ... *midwife* before. Most of the people I am around are students and fellow academics ... an idealistic bunch."

I smile and sip the wine and wonder whose house this is. A sense of nervousness works its way into my brain. I finish the wine.

"You've obviously met the spiritual caretaker ... Stanford's very own confessor," Dr. Miller says and winks at Father Lopez. Lopez ignores this.

"I'm the chaplain for the University's Memorial Church," Father Lopez says. "Dr. Miller and I have had many debates over the years," he says then sips his wine.

There is a burst of laughter, and I notice a well-known painting on one of the walls, *Young Woman in Green*. "Tamara de Lempicka," I say, but more to myself.

Lopez follows my gaze. "It's mesmerizing, isn't it?" he asks.

I nod, but I'm only half paying attention. "The real one is in Paris," I say.

"Sadly," he says nodding, "this one is only a replica. But still."

"Hi," Stanley says walking up to me with a nod to Father

Lopez and Dr. Miller. "Nice party," he adds looking around. "Not the same feel as Haight-Ashbury."

Dr. Miller laughs and says, "Fair enough."

Father Lopez smiles for a few seconds and finally says, "We aren't *that* old."

"Youth and the dawn of life are vanity," Dr. Miller says to Stanley, then looks at Father Lopez and says, "Or so that popular book of *myths* pronounces."

All three of them start talking, something about the frivolity of youth. I mumble "nice to meet you" then walk over to the bar.

Leo looks up at me and smiles, "Interesting crowd," he says.

"I don't feel comfortable here," I say, and I ask the guy behind the bar for a gin.

Leo doesn't say anything. He just keeps time with the music and disappears into his own world.

I walk over to the painting.

I remember my father telling me how it was first displayed in 1930 at the Autumn Salon exhibition in Paris. The style of the painting is Art Deco. There is a profound impression of individuality, of an autonomy trying to escape cultural values through personal expression. Behind the young girl in green is what looks like a metropolitan city, painted in subdued colors and sharp angles. The city is looming. Threatening. There is an indication of unease, of vertigo, a sense of barbed wire draping itself around her, fencing her spirit in societal expectations.

She is wearing a bright green dress that clings to her body, highlighting her curves, her small breasts. Her hands are gloved. White. The fabric running halfway up her forearms. Her left forearm is resting on her upper thigh, holding her dress in place. Her fingers are delicate and have a natural sense of benevolence, peacefulness. She is grasping the brim of her hat as if she is being weather-beaten by heavy gusts. I think of the Santa Ana winds, violent, hot, uncontrolled, raging through the Art Deco buildings in L.A., and this reminds me of my father taking me to the Wiltern Theatre, the Eastern Columbia Building, the Griffith Observatory, the Bullocks Wilshire building, the Jewelry Center, and the Pantages Theatre. I can envision the woman in green standing in front of these buildings, the hot winds battering against her. And there is something, a kind of spiritual tempo, that permeates my mind. I get a vague sense that Christ is somehow whispering to me through these memories, these paintings.

I look at this young woman in gloves, her gaze ... fixated ... a psychological command that absorbs all my attention. I stand back from the painting, trying to get a sense of the overall scene, the tone, and behind her beauty, behind her youth and sexuality, behind the hope that she can protect me, there is a small, quiet sense of sorrow. It's a very soft impression, and in the sorrow, there is a youthful determination that seems to strengthen her femininity, her form.

I get another gin and walk out to the backyard. It's empty, no people around. The back of the house is illuminated in soft white. I sit on a patio chair and light a cigarette. I stare at the circular swimming pool and wonder how much time I need to put in before I can leave without looking rude.

Maybe twenty minutes later, I walk back inside, and Stanley, Dr. Miller, and Father Lopez are still talking. An older woman has joined their conversation. As I walk over to them, I can hear Father Lopez asking Stanley, "So, you are making some kind of documentary?" All four of them look at me as I stand next to Stanley.

"Sami!" Dr. Miller says, slurring a little, "Welcome back. This is Betsy," he says pointing to the older women. Her hair is black and falls down just past her ears. The temples slightly grey. She smiles and shakes my hand.

"Hi," she says.

"Hi."

"She is also a fellow *Cardinal* ... it seems I'm the only Golden Bear here, and I'm completely surrounded," Dr. Miller says and laughs.

Betsy laughs, playing along with the sport rivalry between the two schools.

"Do you teach at Stanford?" I ask.

"No, nothing like that," she says. "I'm the travel coordinator for the athletic department.

I want to tell her about my mom's friend who worked there when I was a kid and all the sports lessons I took, but Father Lopez interrupts before I can say anything.

"I was just asking Stanley about the documentary. What is it about?" Father Lopez asks, also faintly slurring.

"It's about socialism and how the political youth are reaching out to the new left for hope and guidance. It's being made for political science departments for various schools across the nation," I say.

"Interesting ... I wonder what the philosophical reasoning behind their beliefs are?" Father Lopez asks, more to himself.

Dr. Miller looks at Father Lopez, smiles sardonically, and says, "I think Plato has something interesting to say about it ... in the Republic. 'You have forgotten again, my friend, that the law is not concerned to make any one class especially happy, but to ensure the welfare of the commonwealth as a whole. By persuasion or constraint, it will unite the citizens in harmony, making the share whatever benefits each class can contribute to the common good; and its purpose in forming men of that spirit was not that each should be left to go his own way, but that they should be instrumental in binding the community into one.' I personally believe education can help bring about, uh, such a society, which is why I am excited and honored to be a part of the documentary."

"Plato was not a proper socialist, as you know full well," Father Lopez says to Dr. Miller. "He was interested in a philosopher-king, not a Stalin."

"True, true," Dr. Miller says. "But when you get to his ideas concerning the class of producers, there is most certainly strong, hell—undeniable similarities to modern socialism."

"And what is *your* definition of socialism?" Father Lopez asks.

I try not to look at the painting. The room feels hot. I wish I could just sit out back by the pool. I can visualize the metropolitan city scape. I can feel it pressing down on me.

"That's a little difficult ... there are many petals in the rosette of socialism," Dr. Miller says. "You have political aspects; you have economic aspects, and you have social aspects, including ethics, morality ... a kind of anthropocentric fountainhead. In addition to that, you have people that interpret those ideas differently and try to bring them about using different methods. I'm somewhat of an idealist concerning socialism, almost a romantic. I strive for unity, harmony, no crime in the masses."

"I'm curious," Father Lopez says. He pauses for a second. "When you use words like *unity*, *harmony*, and *crime*, doesn't that imply a kind of moral or ethical system?"

"Yes," Miller says.

"Interesting. And where do you get your moral and ethical system from in socialism?" Father Lopez asks.

"What do you mean?" Dr. Miller asks.

"Well, it seems that concepts like morality and ethics imply a standard ... where does this standard come from?" Father Lopez asks.

"I see … well if you are implying a need for religion or belief in God, there is really no point. We get our moral compass from evolution … a sort of baked in safety measure to insure propagation," Dr. Miller replies.

"Morality and ethics are concepts … concepts imply reason … does evolution have reason? Is it an intelligent agent? Does it have a mind?" Father Lopez asks.

"We don't need a God to live right … what we do need is the right socialistic system. We need to ground man in the here and now, not lift his mind up to some false, and ultimately, demeaning spirit," Dr. Miller says.

I think about the young woman in green. I try to imagine what she would think of this conversation. And I can see the hot Santa Anas washing over her. I don't want to be here anymore, I don't want to participate in the futility of this conversation … I don't want to participate in the futility of this life anymore. I pretend I need to use the bathroom and excuse myself.

Later, after leaving the dinner party early, after driving back to my mother's house, I'm sitting in the backyard. It's close to one in the morning. I'm still drinking gin but only sipping it occasionally because I'm already drunk. I briefly wish my mother was here. I wish I could ask her to hug me, to lay next to me on the lounge chair and hold me. An urge to cry washes over me, but I'm not sure if it's because I'm drunk or because I really just want to cry.

And then, I think about Christina and Elisa. I think about the woman riding the horse in the barrel race. I wonder if these women were born in the wrong time. The wrong period. Maybe they don't belong where they are, here, now, in the modern era. They should have lived in the Renaissance age. I think about the painting. I try to focus on the Young Woman In Green. I try to imagine being next to her. I feel a strong wish to rest my head on her lap. A place of safety from the ideological fires that have been burning and burning and burning since 1450. I stare into the lighted pool for what feels like a long time, and I know I will never be able to lay my head on her lap. I start crying. Quietly. And just before I pass out, I think of the orange groves and of my father.

CHAPTER 20

I was just out of college; my father mailed me a newspaper clipping of a car accident. He had cut out the picture but not the article. Underneath the picture, written in small lettering, was the basic information of the car accident. There was nothing else in the envelope, no letter to go along with the picture—nothing but the picture. In the foreground was a violent car accident. Fatal. But in the distant background, there was a stray dog crossing the street. He had circled the dog a bunch of times with a pen, frantically, and next to this, he wrote, "See, I told you so." I didn't understand, didn't know what my father was trying to tell me, didn't comprehend whatever symbolism he was seeing.

CHAPTER 21

It's been a couple of days since the dinner party. I'm in my room at my mom's house. It's a little past midnight, and I'm still somewhat drunk from the gin and the Nembutal I took earlier in the evening. I have a headache, and I'm briefly tempted to look through my mother's medicine cabinet for Dexedrine to take the edge off the gin and Nembutal. But I'm pretty sure she would have taken that with her to Spain. I eventually fall asleep.

"Unimportant," the young-looking lieutenant says. "Maybe one hundred, two hundred residents … average … unimportant." The village sits in a valley near the Laos border. A river coils through the valley. Everything is a variation of green and brown. A Bell UH-1 Iroquois helicopter touches down just outside the village in an area that the lieutenant calls, "The chosen TLZ." Thirteen Army infantrymen jump out of the Huey and run towards the village. It's the fourth helicopter to insert troops. I can hear rifle shots and an occasional grenade. I hold up the camera and walk slowly into the village. Half of it is burning. Some of the Vietnamese men and women are being herded into groups; some are running towards the thick jungle. There is a lot of screaming and shouting and children crying. The sounds are devastating, and I feel slightly nauseous. I don't want to film anymore; I want to ask the young lieutenant to get me out, but then, I see myself filming a soldier. He's standing over the burning body of a child, and he's throwing up. I can hear someone yelling in broken Vietnamese, "Where are the weapons? Where are the weapons?" I turn away from the burning body, and I watch myself as I walk deeper into the village. There is a soldier burning large baskets of rice with a flamethrower.

Next to him are two soldiers smoking cigarettes and chatting, and as I get closer, I can hear them talking about what sports they played in high school. "I wrestled. I was good—not good enough to get a scholarship, but I did well enough … there was a purity in it … you know? I once heard a preacher talk about how God came down and wrestled Jacob in the Old Testament. Now what? I was a wrestler. Where am I? Where's my blessing … I didn't get a new name, a new nature … where's my fucking identity now?"

I walk until I come to a courtyard. There are young kids playing hopscotch and jump rope. An old man and old woman are watching the kids play and crying quietly.

"A generation goes and a generation comes, but the earth remains forever," the young lieutenant whispers to himself, and I'm surprised by the realization that he has been walking with me the whole time. He points to a figure standing a little way off in the shadows of the jungle. I look to where he is pointing. I can see Dionysus, the Greek god of orchards, of wine, of celebration, of sacred frenzy. He's holding a flute in one hand and large wine jug in the other. There is a soldier sitting near him, resting against a large tree that is thick and heavy with ripe mangoes. The solider is mainlining. He looks up at Dionysus, and Dionysus smiles gently at him and starts drinking from the wine jug. The soldier seems abruptly watchful, his eyes darting around, but then his body begins to relax, and around him, yellow trumpetbush, hibiscus, and papaya begin to slowly germinate, growing up around Dionysus and the soldier—his eyes turn glassy.

I briefly wonder if this is how it's always been with wars and the men who had to fight in them, all the way back to antiquity.

"Listen," the young lieutenant says. We both stand still, and I can feel my mind slowly regaining awareness, and through the sluggish mist of waking up, through the sounds of rifles, through the screams, through the crying, through the shouting, through the begging, through the fevered prayers to the gods Thánh Gióng and Liễu Hạnh, I can just hear the solider near Dionysus half singing, half mumbling, "Things fall apart," he sings, his words struggling to get out, "the center cannot hold." There is a long pause, and his head is resting on his chest, "Mere anarchy is loosed upon the world."

CHAPTER 22

Stanley, Leo, and I are at the women's liberation march in Berkeley near the campus. There are thousands of women carrying banners saying, "Women's Liberation," "Equality the time is now," "Women for peace and equality." I've been interviewing one of the organizers of The Women's Liberation Movement for the past half hour, maybe an hour, I'm not really sure. We are all standing on the sidewalk, and Stanley has the woman, whose name I have forgotten, in frame with the march moving behind her. She looks a little younger than me, maybe twenty-three. Twenty-four.

"I don't personally have kids," she's saying, "but I can tell you that women want to contribute to this world apart from being just wives, consumers, and mothers."

I nod appreciatively. "Can you elaborate?" I ask.

"So many women think having kids will fix them—give them meaning and purpose ... identity. That's not really true in the end, especially as kids grow older and don't give the love and affection and meaning women are desperate to get. Desperate. I have talked with a lot of mothers who are completely lost. Our longing for purpose and meaning goes far deeper than a husband or a child. We, as women," she pauses, considering something. "As women in the United States—we are the pioneers for women everywhere but especially in the Western cultures. We have a solemn accountably, a duty and responsibility to live up to the women who fought for years—years—in the Suffrage Movement. They fought for political freedom for women."

I'm nodding and trying to give her my full attention, but there is a daisy growing in the gutter behind her. It's small, and the yellow button in the middle of the flower is bright against the soft, almost silky, white petals.

"Let me ask you a question," she says. "I'll even use the Christianity of our parents as supporting evidence of what we are fighting for." She pauses as someone walking by calls her name. Sandra. Sandra waves and turns back to me. "Do people have sex in heaven?" There is a pause. "Do women give birth in heaven? Are they given in marriage? No, because it's beside the point—I don't believe in heaven or hell or God or Satan, but even their Bible says there's no marriage in heaven."

I try to look contemplative, but I'm focused on the little daisy in the gutter. For some reason, it feels like a sign. Maybe an evolutionary gesture, a symbol of spiritual experience. I almost tell Stanley to film it.

"Women have lost their fundamental identity in raising kids," Sandra says looking directly into my eyes. "In desiring a husband ... a house ... a safe car. Before college, I thought that was what I needed to be, what I was meant for—the newspapers are calling it a baby boom. One of my philosophy professors calls it baby fever ... I don't know what Susan Anthony or Elizabeth Stanton or Lucy Stone would have thought of this boom, but I'm sure they would have rejected the significant cultural pressure to conform to this agenda."

A young man walking by calls out to Sandra and jogs over.

"Hey," he says. "We are heading over to Kathleen and Wayne's after this. Are you coming?"

"Maybe, I don't know," she says.

The young man is standing on the daisy.

"Did you hear about the blow up between the dean and the head of the sociology department?" he asks.

"Yeah, I heard," Sandra says.

"Gotta get back. See you later," the young man says and jogs back to the march. I stare at the crushed daisy.

"Nobody can give me meaning," Sandra continues. "Not a husband, not children. I have to start from myself, must look outward at the world … and seeing no absolute truth, seeing no absolute meaning, I must reach out into the darkness of existence and by an act of the will discover my own meaning in life. You," she says, staring at me again, "should be very troubled by the way our society treats women."

There is a momentary pause.

"So, this movement is about finding meaning?" I ask, trying not to look at the crushed daisy. I light a cigarette, and even though I'm not looking at the daisy, I can see its broken stem, its ruined petals, in my mind. Its beauty ruined, crushed by the foot of man.

"There's such a lack of purpose and meaning for the modern woman," Sandra says. "Women are getting educated—they have goals, desires. But the pressure from society, a society that keeps preaching that women should be homemakers, is putting excessive tension on young women … and the consumerism—that favored child of capitalism is even more aggressive," Sandra says then stops for a moment. "Advertising teaches women that they will be happy and contented only in married life, only in buying goods and raising children, only in supporting their husbands. Only in being attractive little wives."

"So, advertising gives an, uh … fabricated sense of meaning to women?" I ask, trying not to sound mechanical. I wish I could talk to Elisa, and a bizarre hope that she could fix the little daisy engulfs me. I wish I could work in the flower bed with her. I wish we could go on walks together and talk and look out at the green foothills of the Salinas Valley. Billowing clouds drifting across a blue sky.

"As an economical system … I'm, um, not saying capitalism is all bad," Sandra says, and the realization that Elisa doesn't exist, that she is not going show up and take me out of here, almost shatters me.

"—advertising is a kind of psychological violation of women," she continues. "It's adapted to influence women as women … their femininity—I can't explain it as well as some of the sociology professors … there is a very real sexual component to advertising. We, as women, are just there to be pretty and to buy. Advertising is an exploitation of our feminine … uh … instinct."

There is a brief pause, and I try to nod in affirmation. I try to give the unspoken impression that she is doing well and for her to continue explaining the ideas that are motivating the protest.

"There is an abuse of the female predisposition for safety," she says. "They tell us we can have this safety in being a housewife with a clean home full of stuff. But we are resisting this idea, we want to do our own thing—personal expression … autonomy. We decide. Society does not decide for us. Women are treated as sexual objects, told our duty is to be a good, obedient housewife and mother. Obedience. Should our identity really be dependent in such concepts?"

The sound of chanting is loud, and I light another cigarette and wonder where the nearest bar is, and it takes me a few seconds to realize Sandra is looking at me, waiting for me to ask her something. I stare at the clipboard of questions.

"If women feel like sexual objects because of how advertising projects a woman's sexuality … and because of how men, in general, view women … then why doesn't the concept of free love—just basically giving yourself away to anyone, how is that not objectifying?" I ask.

I drag from the cigarette, and I am having a hard time focusing. I start counting backwards from one hundred, hoping to block out the loudness of the march, the noise of thousands of people stretched out for blocks and blocks, the unbroken chanting, my sadness about the daisy—

"Because." She says with a smile, and I suddenly get the impression she has been asked this question before. Probably by her parents.

"We choose who we have sex with. It's not about serving a single person, a husband. Sexual *obligation*. It's *our choice* in who we sleep with and when. We're in control of our sexuality, not men, not society. This is about personal freedom and don't forget—

CHAPTER 23

I t's a few days later. Maybe four. Maybe six. I've isolated myself at my mother's house, and I've been taking Nembutal in the mornings, reading by the pool in the afternoons, and drinking in the evenings—sometimes in the afternoon. I'm pretty sure I missed the interview with Dr. Miller, but neither Leo nor Stanley have called to ask about it.

I'm sitting cross-legged on the edge of the pool. The sun warm against my body. I finished reading the *Girl Scout Handbook* and Virginia Woolf's *A Room of One's Own*. I'm not sure who the *Girl Scout Handbook* belongs to; there's no dedication on the inside. I'm rereading a chapter titled, *The Girl Scout Homemaker*. I briefly wonder what Sandra would say about it. And then I try to remember if I ever gave Stanley or Leo the number to my mother's house.

CHAPTER 24

"Shouldn't we be at the Human Rights March?" Leo asks. We've been filming in the teaching gallery at Stanford's art department for the last hour or so. Father Lopez was able to get me permission to film inside. I look at Leo then at Stanley.

"I need a smoke," Leo mutters. He doesn't have his gear with him. I only want images. No sound.

"I could use a drink," Stanley says, lowering the camera.

"Let's just film a couple more paintings then we can call it a day," I say after a few seconds. "Think of this as ... ideological ... spontaneity." We all look at each other for a few seconds.

"There is a lot more to the flower children than just politics," I finally add. Another brief silence and Stanley shrugs, "Yeah, fuck it. Why not?"

The gallery is extensive and has examples from prehistoric cave drawings all the way up to modern, conceptual art. Some of the works are hand-painted replicas, but most of the gallery is made up of large photographs of the originals.

We stop at a self-portrait of Antonin Artuad. Underneath the photograph is an artwork label giving a few details about Artuad and the date of the work. He was a playwright, a poet, and an essayist. The label lists some of his works, including his play, *To Have Done with the Judgement of God*, and the title of an essay, "Van Gogh: The Man Suicided by Society." Underneath the artwork label is an interpretive label with a quote from *The Republic*. In the quote, Socrates says, "We have discovered that the many conventional notions of the mass of mankind about what is beautiful or honorable or just and so on are adrift in a sort of twilight between pure reality and pure unreality."

"Wait," Leo says, then, in a tone that suggests he's just realizing something, "take the rest of the day off ... does that mean we aren't going to film the Human Rights march after this?"

Next to the self-portrait of Artuad is a massive photograph of Jay DeFeo's, *The Rose*. Written on the artwork label is "The Rose 1958-66. Oil on canvas with wood and mica." And underneath is a quote from Thomas Merton that reads, "Most people only experience beauty as if in a dream ... ultimate beauty approached in this life is rare."

"Let's get a drink," I say and read the quote again. Then again. There is something suggestive about the words, "as if in a dream," something overriding. Tenderly. A metaphysical sincerity. An image of soft blue water suddenly fills my mind so completely, so viscerally, that I can actually feel myself being submerged, feel the delicate pressure of the water against my body, feel the lightness of my body floating. I can see sunlight glittering on the surface, penetrating the water, creating beautiful patterns of dappled light. A sense of warmth begins to permeate my body. I'm so consumed by the image and the warmth that I only dimly register that I'm saying, "Then, we can drive up to San Francisco and film the march."

CHAPTER 25

"Sami!" Autumn calls from across the room. She is throwing another large party. Woodrow Guthrie's "This Land Is Your Land" is playing on the record player.

"Sami," Autumn calls again and makes her way over to me. She smiles and hugs me. "How's the documentary coming along?"

"It's okay," I say, looking around the busy living room. "Where are Stanley and Leo?"

"Last I saw, they were in the backyard. Catching some rays. Leo's on his own thing. Shrooms. Really mellow," Autumn says. "Why just okay?"

"I could use a drink," I say, lighting a cigarette.

Autumn gives me another hug, "You seem down. Want a bennie?"

"No thanks, just a drink."

"We have wine and beer," she offers.

I'm standing in the backyard an hour later, sipping from my third glass of wine. Leo is shirtless and stretched out on a bench. His eyes are closed, but he's been smiling nonstop for the last thirty minutes.

"Thomas called ... he's a little upset we didn't go to the interview with Dr. Miller," Stanley is saying.

I look at him but don't respond.

"I told him I was sick with a stomach bug that day and couldn't get out bed ... he accepted that, but I got the impression he thought it was a cop out ... since we didn't call Dr. Miller and inform him ... of the situation ... or reschedule," he says and starts to chuckle.

I smile, lighting another cigarette.

"You didn't have to do that," I say and sip the wine. "But thanks for covering for me."

"No sweat."

Autumn walks up to us. She's with a young woman, maybe twenty-two. The woman is wearing a beautiful, bright-red, knitted poncho that comes down to a point just past the waistband of her well-worn blue jeans. No belt. No shoes. The poncho is semi-see through, and she is not wearing anything underneath. Her hair is chestnut brown and naturally wavy, long enough to reach her chest. Her bangs are messy, side swept.

"Hi, Sami," Autumn says. "This is Sierra—I was telling her about the documentary you are making."

"Hi," Sierra says, looks me full in the eyes, and smiles. Her eyes are hazel; her features delicate. She hugs Stanley and me, and I'm a little surprised by the warmth of her body.

"She lives across the Golden Gate, Mill Valley," Autumn says. "Her parents own a large amount of property up there. Bedrock."

"My parents named it Bedrock before I was born," Sierra adds. "So the documentary is about political activism?"

"Yes. It's mostly an educational film," I say.

"Intended for political science departments ... at various universities," Stanley says.

"Leo and Stanley were telling me you filmed the gallery in the Stanford art department a few days ago," Autumn says.

I nod. "It's a really good gallery. Very extensive. My father took me there several times. When I was young. He wanted me to appreciate the value of art, of beauty."

"Is that also for the documentary?" Sierra asks.

"No," I say. "Not directly, anyway."

"The political activism can be somewhat ... repetitious," Stanley says.

"You should come stay at Bedrock," Sierra says. "We have a small community on the property. There's plenty of room." "Ode to Billie Joe" by Bobbie Gentry is playing on the radio. "You could film there if you want. A different cultural perspective from the politics."

CHAPTER 26

I was 12 or 13. I had woken up in the middle of the night, thirsty. I was walking to the bathroom to drink from the faucet when I heard my father's voice from the kitchen. I walked downstairs and stood in the doorway.

My parents were in the kitchen. My father was trying to explain something to my mother. She had asked him a question. Even though I stood in the kitchen doorway, they didn't notice me. He was silent, breathing softly, a drink in his hand. Then quietly, almost to himself, "I'm having trouble following the ideas ... there was a man walking in the cemetery ... cutting himself with sharp stones ... the Santa Ana's were strong today. The palms were bending violently. It was ... hypnotizing. I was reminded of that movie we were producing back then. The set was closed, an effort to create ... strong ... we watched as he annihilated her bedroom, trying to break free from disillusionment—I can't stop thinking about the palm's bending ... with that film, we were trying to accomplish a great sound, but nothing was really heard ... it was ... just a film based on a desire for revenge, a way to lash out at an idea. We were rejecting opulence. But we were all hypocrites. We couldn't look each other in the eye after that *scene. What lunatic has ever risen above the institution that held him—even if, from time to time, he apprehended an extreme perception, extreme clarity? What difference does it really make in the end—from a technical point of view, there was really nothing new. Painters, for hundreds of years, were doing everything we could with a camera. Chiaroscuro lighting, focus, jump cuts, center of reference ... these had an aesthetic effect, but nothing was really being said. Truth no longer holds ... call to me, and I will answer and show you great and unsearchable things you do not know. Anthropocentric attitudes are ... inherently obscure; truth is not desired ... escaping futility, guilt, boredom is the only craving. These things were established in the city of Enoch. Pierre Auguste's work ... there must be more to this life," he said.*

He kept talking, and my mother quietly cried.

CHAPTER 27

I'm standing out in front of a small bar in downtown San Francisco, smoking a cigarette. Stanley and Leo are in the bar playing pool. I'm humming the words to "This Land Is Your Land." I smoke two more cigarettes before finally walking back into the bar. I order a gin, my fourth, and sit back down on the stool. The bar is dark and empty apart from Leo, Stanley, me, and a man and woman sitting together at the other end of the bar.

"Drown yourself," a man's voice says behind me. I turn around, but there is no one there and I have to fight hard not to scream, not to scream back at the voice.

Stanley says something to Leo about Leo's last shot, and Leo laughs.

I turn back to the bar, and I can hear voices whispering, and I'm having a hard time concentrating. The gin soothes my brain, warms my chest, reassuring me, and I don't feel afraid of the whispering, but I can't seem to focus. I start counting the liquor bottles, hoping for clarity, for direction.

I try to backtrack in my mind; I was out front smoking a cigarette. But you can smoke in the bar, I tell myself. I notice that the bartender is staring at me and slowly realize I was talking out loud. I start counting to fifty in my mind … trying to snap back into the moment. Then, I remember the song and start humming, and it becomes important to remember the words, but I don't know why. I get to fifty. Nothing happens. I light a cigarette, and then I remember the words, " … the sun came shining ... and I was strolling … and the wheat fields waving and the dust clouds rolling," I murmur, and something like hope pours into me, a way back, a way back to clarity and meaning.

"This land was made for you and me."

CHAPTER 28

My brother is floating on the bottom of a swimming pool. His eyes are open, and he is staring into nothingness. I want to jump into the pool and rescue him, but I can't move. Then, I'm floating face down in the pool, my hair spilling out around me, my dress gently moving in the water. I wake up. It's dark. I'm in my room at my mother's house.

CHAPTER 29

"Sami," a voice says. There is a long pause.

"Sami," the man says again, and I recognize the sound of my father's voice over the phone. I don't remember calling him. It's a little after eleven in the evening.

"Are you listening?"

"Yes," I say. I can tell he's drunk, and he's telling me about his brother, my uncle, Rick. Rick was a cop. Rick shot himself in the head in the Mojave Desert before I was born.

"Signs and wonders," he says. "Transfiguration ... exquisite beauty ... our family is afflicted ... your grandfather was institutionalized ... for a year," he says, and there is a pause. I can hear the sound of ice cubes rattling in glass through the phone.

"I was ten at the time," he says. "I remember missing him."

"I'm struggling ... with the documentary," I say nervously, my voice faintly shaky.

"Frenetic—what happened to the mind of man? Meaningless ... utterly empty. Emptiness in the Santa Ana winds ... that drive flames across the mountains of Southern California ... emptiness in a 6.5 earthquake ... emptiness in dry clouds ... emptiness in *entire generations lost and fighting to come to terms ... with this emptiness," he says. There is another long pause.*

"I'm ... struggling ... a little bit with the documentary ... I'm drawn to the counterculture's effort to get back to nature ... beauty ... back to the spiritualism of the old world ... I know it's a political film ... I don't know ... I don't know what to do ... I just feel a desire to see the beauty of this moment, to feel its depth, to experience its meaning," I say. There is another long pause, and my heart is beating fast, and I am hoping he will say something, encourage me. Tell me he misses me.

"I don't understand this descendant ... of Abraham," he says, but he's no longer talking to me.

A sense of hopelessness slams into me.

"I don't understand ... why Christ?" he asks. "Why Jesus ... Hebrew of Hebrews ... can't you help me ... you say you are a liberator. Why did you let us destroy the land? Why did you let us destroy the orange groves ... the center cannot hold—Sami," he says.

I don't respond. I don't say anything.

"The center cannot hold," he says, his words slurring.

"I'm lonely," I say. "I miss you."

He is humming now, the alertness gone.

"Where are you?" I ask. More silence.

"The. Center. Cannot. Hold."

"Where are you?" I ask, on the verge of crying.

"What?" he asks, his words slow, heavy.

"Where are you?"

Silence.

"In set ... on set ... in Texas."

"That's not what I mean ... I don't know where you are anymore ... I miss you," I say. But he does not hear me anymore.

"Why did this Moshiach, this Christ, let my son drown?" he says, the sounds of his crying hard now, open weeping.

CHAPTER 30

A week later, Stanley, Leo, and I drive to the Bedrock property in Mill Valley, about thirty minutes north of San Francisco. The property sits at the end of Fern Canyon Road in the foothills of Mount Tamalpais State Park. The dirt driveway has been widened to accommodate about twenty vehicles. There are three cars, a Volkswagen Van, and a station wagon parked in the driveway.

We get out of the van and look at the main house—two floors with large wrap-around decks on both the lower and upper floor. Stanley lights a cigarette. Frank Sinatra's version of "Fly Me to the Moon" is playing from the house.

"Smell that?" Stanley asks, taking a drag from his cigarette. "Someone is baking fresh bread."

People are sitting and hanging out on both decks. A man wearing only blue jeans is playing a small flute to the music, and although I can't see them, I can hear children laughing and shouting. Sierra is sitting in one of the rocking chairs on the bottom deck. She waves at us and then walks over, holding a joint. Three dogs get up and walk with her, their tails wagging happily. A black lab, a beagle and a German shepherd.

"Hi Sami," she says brightly. She hugs me then looks at Leo and Stanley. "Hi," she says to them and hugs them.

"Frank Sinatra?" I ask. She looks at me for a moment, slightly puzzled. "Oh, the music," she says, takes a hit off the joint, exhales. "Yeah, we're an eclectic bunch here." A young girl, maybe ten, runs from the back of house, laughing. She is wearing a yellow t-shirt, blue jeans, and a head wreath made of oak leaves.

"Nice place," Leo says, looking around. "Really pretty."

Sierra nods. "Yeah, my folks are … understanding. We have nine cabins throughout the property … a vegetable garden, three cows—I'll introduce you to the animals later. We also have a small pottery studio, an art studio, and even a woodworking shop … we like to experiment with different forms of expression." There is a brief pause. "We have a cabin for you, but only the main house has electricity and indoor plumbing," she says. "We're about unrestricted humanity, sharing, working together, love, artistic expression … I'm glad you took me up on my offer to come visit. You are welcome to stay as long as you like. I already told everyone you might show up and a little about the documentary you are making. They're cool with it … but please leave any hang-ups back in society," Sierra says with a smile. And as she leads us to our cabin Ella Fitzgerald and Louis Armstrong are singing, "Cheek to Cheek."

CHAPTER 31

The afternoon sun is bright and warm. I'm floating on my back in a small creek that moves through the eastern side of the property. Someone, I forget who, named it the "New Euphrates," adding that the commune is the "cradle of a new kind of civilization." The water is cold and flows around me. My eyes are closed, and I'm focusing on the effects of the water on my body, attempting to empty my mind. The sounds of the creek passing over small stones is pleasant, calming. My dress sits heavy against my body, lightly pushing me against the shallow bottom.

After an hour, maybe longer, I walk back to our cabin. I can hear someone strumming on a guitar and signing softly ... languidly. "The city that sits solitary, captured in her dream."

We've been at the commune for five days.

CHAPTER 32

I'm sitting with a small group of young men and women on the upper deck of the house. Stanley, Leo, and I have been filming the interior and exterior of the main house, the art studio, and some of the cabins and animals, attempting to capture the atmosphere of the commune. This is the first day that we have actually done any filming, and I'm hoping that the people at the commune are accustomed to our presence and feel comfortable around us.

Leo is running sound, and Stanley is filming the small group. Someone in the house has put on Dizzy Gillespie. I've only asked the group a couple of questions, not wanting to interrupt the natural flow of their discussions, wanting them to be as true to themselves as possible. There is a kind of beauty in listening to them, listening to their laughter and delight. Sometimes, they are quiet, and sometimes, the conversation gets heavy.

A young girl named Linda is quietly tapping her fingers to the music. "You know," she says looking up, "it's interesting ... but in some ways the teachings of Buddha and the teaching of existential crisis are the same," she pauses. "I don't fully understand it ...

but from what I've read, suffering is unavoidable and even to be embraced … as a way through the suffering, to be free … in existentialism, meaninglessness is unavoidable and the way through this is acceptance—build meaning through an act of the will—The Four Noble Truths teach that suffering comes from strong affection to things, to pleasure." Another pause. "Freedom from suffering comes through giving up these strong affections … don't they seem similar?" she finishes. There is a brief silence as the group thinks about this.

"Still though," a young man, who calls himself Orion—I think Leo told me his birth name is Jack—says, "I definitely don't want to give up pleasure."

The group laughs, and someone else says, "We should take a trip," and there is a murmur of agreement.

Later, around nine in the evening, Stanley and I are sitting in a couple rocking chairs on the bottom deck, drinking and smoking cigarettes. The radio in the house is playing KMPX-FM with "Big Daddy" Donahue. Leo is on a trip with Linda and Orion and a few others. There is a faint smell of sandalwood incense and fresh bread coming from the house. The German shepherd, named Wanderer, is sleeping next to Stanley. I wonder what Meria would say about giving a name to the dog.

"Why didn't you interview them?" Stanley asks.

I sip from a can of Coors.

Donahue's deep voice, in a brief talk-over, starts "Somebody to Love" by Darby Slick and sung by Grace Slick, both of whom Donahue explains, were members of the band the Great Society. "The song's original title was 'Someone to Love' and was written by Darby while he was going through a breakup."

"I want this place … this moment in time … to be real … we've met our fair share of plastic hippies in San Francisco … I didn't want to steer the conversation ... I'm tired of setting an agenda. I just want to see how it really is," I say.

"But in your head, baby, I'm afraid you don't know where it is," Grace sings.

CHAPTER 33

I'm standing in the art studio. Alone. It's early afternoon, and the sun is bright in the clear blue sky. I haven't slept in almost two days. Hanging on one of the walls are two replica paintings of works by Henry Ossawa Tanner, *The Banjo Lesson* and *The Annunciation*. I've been staring at the paintings, intermittently, for the last forty-eight hours. *The Banjo Lesson* depicts an old man teaching a young boy how to play the banjo. The room they're in is old, bare, with just the mere basics to be livable. The old man and young boy live in deep, deep poverty, and in the center of this poverty are the old man and young boy. The contrast of the room and the attention of the young boy with the banjo brings into focus the idea of one generation trying to pass on beauty, through artistic skill, to the next generation. A beauty that some-how, set against the backdrop of poverty, strengthens the beauty. Makes the beauty a solid thing.

I look at *The Annunciation*. A feeling of devastation flows through me. I study Mary. She is sitting on the side of her bed, looking at the angel Gabriel. The look on her face is difficult for me to interpret. She is not facing Gabriel head-on; her body and face are slightly turned away, and there is the idea that she is realizing the absolute beauty and power in Gabriel. But her eyes, clear, are not turned away from Gabriel like the rest of her body. Gabriel appears at the foot of her bed as a ray of light rather than an actual angelic being in complete form.

I briefly wonder if he is intentionally appearing to her with enough distance between them so as not to make her feel over-whelmed ... or threatened by him. The painting makes me feel like I am interrupting something I should not see. Something that is only meant for Mary. The painting makes me hold my breath and makes me desperate for an angel to appear to me. The room Mary is in also gives a sense of poverty but not as intense as the room in *The Banjo Lesson*. Beauty in the midst of poverty.

When I had asked Sierra about the paintings, she said a young teenage boy from Alabama, who stayed at the property in December, brought the paintings with him when he came out west. "I think he might have stolen them from the small public library in his town," she said. "He seemed to imply that anyway."

At some point in the last two days, I had gone into town to the liquor store and bought three bottles of gin—at some point, I called my mother.

"It's one in the morning here, Sami," she said.

"When are you coming home? You've been gone a long time," I say.

"I'll be home in a couple of days. I promise. Is everything okay?"

"I just wanted to give you the number where I'm staying. I'm in Mill Valley ... I can't reach my father. Will you please give him my number?"

"Sami ... "

"I'm sorry for waking you up ... again. Bye."

CHAPTER 34

There is a sense of something speeding up in my mind, an idea that is trying to rush through to the forefront of my thoughts. The days seem ... fast ... I'm having difficulty keeping track of the movements, keeping track of the purpose, keeping track of the themes. I am tormented by a desperate need to see my father ... to hear his voice in person. To see him face to face. I wish my father would hug me, reassure me—

CHAPTER 35

I was eight or nine; my father was holding my hand. We were walking to Werry Park in Palo Alto. His hand was warm, strong, comforting. The sky was filled with thick, rolling clouds. My mother argued with my father. She did not want us to go out in the stormy weather; she was nervous, worried about my father for some reason I didn't understand.

"I don't want to do this anymore," he said to her. We were in the kitchen, and I was standing next to him, holding his hand, waiting for him to take me to the park.

"Don't leave," she said.

"I feel trapped ... caught in something, maybe Couture's *The Romans ... in their ... Decadence. I can't seem to get out,*" he said. She didn't respond. And after a few seconds of silence he said, quietly, "I don't want to do this anymore."

"I know."

It wasn't until a few years ago, in my early twenties, that I learned he wasn't talking about their relationship, their marriage. "He didn't want to be ... in this world anymore," my mother had told me.

The clouds held a deep darkness in certain places. The wind

was gentle at first and brushed across my face, but later, it picked up speed. The park was empty, and I let go of my father's hand and ran to the swings. My father sat at a wooden picnic table nearby. I loved the sensation of my body pushing back and forth, picking up speed, kicking my legs out in front of me on the upswing. There was the rush of floating in my stomach as I swung up and the sense of falling sending a burst of excitement as I came back down. The clouds were getting darker, heavier, and I could smell water in the air. The wind was picking up speed with strong gusts crashing into me, whipping my hair across my face.

CHAPTER 36

Sierra is throwing a party at Bedrock that has been going, non-stop, for three days with no sign of slowing down. People have been dropping in, some staying the night, others leaving the same day. On the second day, there were almost two hundred people. Men. Women. Children. Pets. I stopped counting the camping tents when I got to thirty.

In one of the fields behind the property is a tall maypole. On top of the maypole is an elaborate bouquet of California wildflowers. Surrounding the maypole is a circle of boys and girls. All the children have a crown of daisies on their heads. They are each holding a brightly-colored ribbon in their hands, and the other end of the ribbon is attached to the top of the maypole. They are dancing while moving in a circle around the maypole. Their ribbons begin to weave into a tight pattern around the pole as they continually move in a circle.

"It's not May," Stanley says to me without taking his eye away from the camera's viewfinder. I don't say anything. Leo is walking around, recording sounds of music, of laughter, of conversations.

I remember a children's book my father read to me and my brother when we were young. In the book were four fairies, each holding a ribbon tied to an apple tree. They were dancing in a circle, and they each were wearing a dress representing the four seasons: green, red, blue, and pink. I look at the children dancing around the maypole and wish I had a high-speed camera so I could film them and play it back in slow motion.

"We're getting good footage … nice turnout," Stanley says.

Later that day, Leo, Stanley, and I are at the ceramic shop filming mothers and a couple of fathers as they teach about fifteen children how to make pottery. After about twenty minutes, I leave Stanley and Leo and walk out into the bright sunlight. I light a cigarette and stand still, listening to the sounds of children laughing, music playing, and cars driving in and out of the property. I walk to our cabin and pour myself a gin and sit on the edge of the bed. I finish the gin and pour another. I want Nembutal, but I decide against it since I wouldn't be able to conduct interviews if I took Nembutal on top of the gin. I'm tempted to look for Wanderer; I'm tempted to strip and float in the creek; I'm tempted to play hide and seek with the kids; I'm tempted to get in my car and drive to L.A.; I'm tempted to call Thomas and tell him I'm not interested in making a film about politics.

As I walk out of the cabin, I notice three girls sitting underneath a large oak tree. They are sitting Indian style, their knees touching and their hands resting on their knees. I watch them for a few minutes. A strange hunger—an emotional need—a desire for psychological comfort begins to slowly overtake me, and I have to fight off the desire for Nembutal. I walk over to them, and they look up at me and smile warmly.

"Do you want to join us?" one of the young women asks me.

"What are you doing?" I ask.

"We're practicing meditative yoga," she says and pointing to each of the young women in turn. "Hollie is practicing Bhakti yoga, and Meadow practices pagan worship, the old beliefs. Folklore. She is in love with a Goddess, a divinity that represents femininity—but she also believes in animism, all things have a spiritual value to them."

"And what about you?" I ask.

"I'm Ophelia. I practice—no—I *surrender* to the beauty of Eastern mysticism," she says.

Stanley and Leo walk over to me. I've asked Ophelia a question, and she is answering me. But the gin is warm in my stomach, and I can almost feel the alcohol, absorbing, moving in my blood stream, pouring into my brain.

Ophelia is saying, "It's more about letting go of value systems … it's transcending all things, although all things can help you to let go. Suffering—not having a sense of self-awareness or belonging—you have to let go of a sense of self." She closes her eyes for a minute then opens them again. "Love will free you. Our parents say we are crazy, but just think about it. What if everyone loved each other?"

I try to think about this. I think of evil and selfishness. I think of crime and try to imagine everyone loving each other. I tell myself it's beautiful. I tell myself I could be there—in the wide-open fields. Stanley motions to ask me if he should start filming, and I nod my head. And then I notice a little girl dancing and spinning in circles. Next to her is a man without a shirt, and he is dancing in place and holding a beer. He has yellow flowers in his hair. Someone has dragged the couch out of the main house and placed it on the bottom deck of the house, and five women are sitting on the couch, drinking, and talking, and laughing. One of the women passes a joint to the girl sitting next to her. And then Stanley and Leo are filming a family living out of a small, converted school bus.

I can feel the Nembutal calming me down, but I don't remember taking it.

Sitting by the back of the school bus are seven young children, three boys and four girls. A young woman is giving them pieces of bread with raspberry jam. She holds up a camera and takes a picture of them. The children giggle, and I'm walking out into a field where a vegetable garden has been planted.

A woman is watering the vegetables and someone is asking, "Do you like Allen Ginsberg?"

And someone answers, "he is a great poet ... *Howl* was so influential for me. His generation showed us that our parents are apathetic and living in anxiety ... I also like Arthur Rimbaud, Walt Whitman, Henry Miller—they are trying to give meaning by looking for the beatific vision in the gutters of humanity ... finding God sitting next to the drunk passed out in an alleyway ... they felt a sense of alienation from the culture they were living in. Just like us. I think it has to do with Transcendentalism. You know, like, love for the environment, feminism, communal living. It's not a new belief system. It's rather old ... can you imagine ... seeing the face of God? All anxiety would just vanish. Our culture is lost. Our parents are trying to find meaning in strict order, moral rigidity."

Someone has attached an amplifier and large speakers to a record player and "Dear Mr. Fantasy" by Traffic is booming out from the main house, and someone is explaining to me that the record is bootlegged. I'm standing in one of the cabins. On a bed are four young girls between the ages of three and nine. All four have dirty blonde hair and brown eyes. Their mother, who calls herself Gypsy, is sitting between the girls. She is wearing a man's shirt. Unwashed. The father, Marley, is sitting in a chair next to the bed. He is only wearing a pair of jeans. He is reading *In a Myrtle Shade* by William Blake. I think I remember my dad telling me William Blake was a poet who influenced the beatniks.

And I'm walking down a trail that leads to a large field with tall, wild oat grass and flowers. The colors are surreal. Dark orange, bright yellow, soft purple. I hear laughter and look around. I notice a group of young children walking through the field, almost completely obscured by wild oat. "I've had a final experience ... I've had a final experience," someone is saying.

My mind is anesthetized. I'm crying. I wish Autumn was here. I wish she would hug me. The ground is dissolving beneath me. A terror is on my heart. I can't stop crying. I desperately look for someone to rest my head upon, but I see only a profound confusion. The shouting in my mind is too loud. I cover my ears with my hands. "Can you hear it?" I scream. But there is no one there. No one comes running. Just behind the screams is a terrible stillness, a foreboding in which the dread ... the screaming in my mind suddenly explodes into an unexpected and overwhelming sense of awe ... a kind of spiritual supernova. I am unable to control what I see in these moments. Rossetti's *Ecce Ancilla Dominie—Behold the Handmaiden of The Lord*. The Angel Gabriel appearing to Mary. I sense an overwhelming desire to see what Mary saw. There is a strange apprehension in Mary's face.

I stare out the window for hours. The sky is filled with heavy clouds, pregnant with blackness and deep blues, a brief sunlight illuminates the clouds far away, clouds on the distant horizon. Clouds that carry an idea ... I cannot seem to form the idea clearly in my mind. There is a suggestion in the darkness of the clouds, a kind of reading, like a living painting. I was taught to read a painting from right to left, to focus on the point of convergence. I see myself crawling along the gutters of San Francisco.

"I can't reach my father. He won't return my calls."

"It's all in your mind ... you need to let go," a woman's voice says, and I think about Andrea Mantegna's *The Lamentation of Christ*. I can see the painting in my mind, and I am transfixed by its terrible beauty; there is no divine repose, no Mary to hold his body; instead, the body of Christ is laying on a bed. His skin grey, lifeless. There is an expression of agony on his face as though he died in pain, a spiritual lamentation that only he could face. The wounds in his hands and feet are clearly visible, and the painting of his corpse gives off the idea that he could easily be laying in the morgue. I wonder if I would have filmed him if he had died in the modern era. He is called the man of sorrows, giving the impression that there is an aesthetic value rooted in his suffering. A value I chase, a value I try to capture on film, in interviews, in ideology, in the land. There is a kind of freedom in this sorrow, this aesthetic ... in the nature of beauty. Freeing me from the anthropocentric ideology that I am the point of my life.

"Sami ... are you listening to me?" the woman asks.

"Why won't he call me? When is he coming back home?"

"Sami ... honey ... it's all in your mind," my mother is saying over the phone, and I feel myself falling. "Your father's ... dead ... it's been two years," she says gently, and I barely register her voice anymore. I want to scream, but instead, I just begin crying.

"He's not coming back," she says.

CHAPTER 37

My father and I would go for long drives together throughout my adolescent and early teen years. Sometimes, he would take me to the Santa Ana Valley. He would park in the hills, and we would look out at the sprawling landscape of orange groves. Sometimes, he would try to explain to me the meaning of rural farming, of the beauty and value of men and women working the ground.

Sometimes, he would get out of the car and sit on the hood and stare out at the rows and rows of orange trees. The trees were green against the dark earth. I would watch him from the front seat of the car. He had dirty-blonde hair and grey-blue eyes. And when he would sit on the hood looking out at the valley below, a feeling would flow through me. I wanted to be where he was, see what he was seeing, the indication, the rhythm, a lament only he seemed to hear. "The land is screaming ... crying out," he once told me, but I didn't really understand.

Sometimes, his shoulders would gently shake, and I knew he was crying, and I wanted to put my arms around him and tell him not to worry. I wanted to rescue him. But instead, I just sat in the *front seat of the car, blushing from the shame—the sense of disgrace that I would never be able to help him. Over time, the valley changed from groves to urban housing. He would take me out there less and less.*

Eventually, we stopped going.

CHAPTER 38

The party at Bedrock is still going. I think it's been two days since the call with my mother. I'm sitting in a wicker chair in my cabin. I'm alone and sipping from my fourth or fifth gin. On a small nightstand, that I moved next to the chair, are two Nembutal and a sharp pruning knife that I got from the garden shed. I'm smoking a cigarette with slow deliberation, focusing on the way the tobacco feels as it fills my lungs. I can hear people laughing. Bob Dylan's "Like a Rolling Stone" is playing from the house, and people are singing along. Every once in a while, I hear children shouting joyfully.

I feel oddly calm as I take the two Nembutal. I sip the gin and wait for the first indications that the drug has entered my bloodstream. Ten minutes pass. "Heroin" by The Velvet Underground is playing when the gradual sedation begins to form in my brain, and as I cut my wrist open with the pruning knife, I wonder if Thomas is going to use the footage.

CHAPTER 39

" ... **S**ymptoms are indictive of the manic-depressive condition," a man is saying to my mother. "You may have noticed that when she is manic her mood is elevated to the point of euphoria ... talking rapidly, acting more gregarious. Racing thoughts. Auditory hallucinations. Visual hallucinations ... related to the mania—it's important to understand that when she is like this, what she hears, what she sees is very vivid ... very real to her. Most people don't understand this ... they don't realize how real these visual and audible delusions can be. Then, her mood will swing violently toward depression. In this state, she can become almost catatonic. She won't do anything. Just sleep. She won't take care of her body—won't bathe, won't eat. There's one more thing ... in her manic state ... she experiences religious delusions ... she believes she is having spiritual experiences. This is fairly common. We want to put her on Haldol, but for now, we're keeping her on Thorazine."

There's a long pause. "She's extremely lucky that one of her crew members found her ... before she was beyond all help."

Another pause. "I'm having difficulty getting any information about her family history, especially as it concerns her father. She hasn't really talked about him. But she has mentioned a house in Los Angeles a few times."

"That's her father's house ... *was* her father's house," my mother says. "She was his only beneficiary. The house is hers."

"So her father is dead," the man asks and writes something down on a clipboard he is holding.

"Yes ... two years ago ... in Texas—working on a film. The day the picture wrapped, he went to his hotel room and shot himself," my mother says hesitating. There is a long silence as the man writes. "And her little brother drowned when she was sixteen," she says. "But ... Sami keeps acting like he's still alive ... her father I mean ... she ... talks to him."

Another long silence as the man continues to take notes.

"That can be alarming to see," he says sounding sympathetic, "but talking to loved ones who have passed is a fairly common feature of grief. It's well-known but not well-studied. It's sometimes referred to as bereavement hallucinations—there are a few references to this phenomenon over the last one hundred years. People have even experienced these hallucinations with a beloved pet that has passed. I need more information about her family history—"

"That's fine, but right now I want to talk to her," my mother says, cutting him off.

"That's fine ... you should know that Thorazine may cause her to have difficulty in thinking ... she may be slow or possibly unresponsive."

The bench I'm sitting on creaks for a moment as mother sits down next to me. She gently tucks my hair behind my ear with her fingers then holds my hands.

"Mom ... where am I?" I manage to ask, but my thoughts are slow, and my words trickle out.

"Agnew's ... it's a special hospital."

"How ... how ... long have I been ... here?"

"Not too long. But don't worry, you can go home soon ... they just want to make sure you get the right medication ... to help you," she says and then pauses. "—Oh, I almost forgot—your friend Stanley got in touch with me. He wanted me to tell you that Thomas is going to use all the footage you took."

"Does ... Dad know where I am?"

"Do you understand you tried to harm yourself?"

Many religious experiences are inextricably aesthetic—few, indeed, could be called purely spiritual or intellectually theological { ... } the Pseudo-Dionysian notion of a hierarchy of beauty: from corporeal and sensible beauty the mind is drawn upward to contemplation of itself as their perceiver, and to its own spiritual beauty and the beauty of intelligible form; and these, finally are seen as dependent on and participating in the highest beauty, which is also the highest Art, interior to mind and also above it, the cause of all beauty.

— Richard Viladesau

For my father
1949-2020

From left to right: me, my father, my brother.

ACKNOWLEDGMENTS

I found my way to Mike Carson's hazy realism paintings about a decade ago, and I am honored that he gave me permission to use his *Blue Window* as the cover for this book. His art depicts humanity in a way that deeply moves me. You can find him on Instagram, @mcarson1999 and his website is mikecarson.art.

Laurel and I are grateful to the editing and formatting expertise for this book by Andi Cumbo of Mountain Ash Press. Her guidance, particularly about the correct punctuation for all the paintings and songs I reference, was of tremendous value. She also helped me to give greater depth to Sami.